Conspirator's Odyssey

Conspirator's Odyssey
The Evolution of the Patron Saint

*   *   *

A.K. Kuykendall

www.intoprintpublishing.com

Kuykendall, A.K.
Conspirator's Odyssey: The Evolution of the Patron Saint
228 p. 1.33 cm.
ISBN 978-1-62352-000-7 (Perfect Bound)
ISBN 978-1-62352-001-4 (EPub)

1. Suspense -- Fiction 2. Science Fiction 3. Conspiracies -- United States -- Fiction

Revised Edition

To my wife, Magdiel Kuykendall. In the decades, days, hours, minutes, and seconds in my life, the most momentous was—and always will be—the evening we met.

AUTHOR'S NOTE

As a young man and a United States Marine Corps brat for the better part of my existence, I grew up with the smell of fatigues, which lingered regularly about the many bases my family and I both visited and resided—the pungent aroma trailing me as I made my way through life.

Along with my cravings, bordering on the obsessive, for ready-to-eat military stock meals (MRE's) I was brought up to appreciate the military's code of conduct. On the other side of the coin and through my days I was especially diligent in historic readings, literature of all genres, and with the media goings-on in the world, all witnessed from an obscure perch I dubbed *Forte Kuykendall.* As the days in my life ticked by and as history played itself out before my eyes, I continually found myself at a loss for words in reflection of the many tempestuous global occurrences.

There was entirely too much upheaval in the world and I couldn't get my head around it all. This is when I decided to prioritize and I allowed my passions to take hold. And though I was born eleven years after his assassination, the late John F. Kennedy became my focus and with this came a torrent of mysterious doors I instinctively knew neither I nor anyone else was meant to open.

In reflection of my time as a military brat witnessing repeat deployments on behalf of our nation, from what I had discovered; I was then and still am to this very day floored by the rampant political corruption that has covertly reduced our American soldiers to blind defenders and lambs for the slaughter.

In searching for answers through an extensive research process, a highly complex picture began to emerge with both eerie and true-to-life connections. And in my desperate need to make sense of it all I pushed on exhaustively researching every angle that emerged and then I made a connection that, at first, even I could hardly believe. I discovered the true meaning behind former President Dwight David Eisenhower's January 17, 1961 farewell address to the nation. By playing on the complexities within my own research, I decided to use the very same historical information that led to this discovery to present a plausible backdrop and Conspirator's Odyssey was born.

As it is written in Wikipedia, *"a conspiracy theory explains an event as being the result of an alleged plot by a covert group or organization or, more broadly, the idea that important political, social or economic events are the products of secret plots that are largely unknown to the general public."* And so I chose to present my story in the trend of The Illuminatus Trilogy.

I made it a point to paint an all-too-believable picture of interconnecting, power-hungry, conspiratorial madmen who essentially run the nation behind the scenes. But while Illuminatus is scatterbrained and nearly impossible for the average reader to follow, *Conspirator's Odyssey* gradually blossoms to reveal each new layer and fold at just the right pace.

THE ANCHOR [?]

It all began for our nation on July 4, 1947 at the Roswell Army Air Base when General Roger Ramey briefed President Harry S. Truman on the incident.

"It was more than a blip on our radar screens that we witnessed yesterday evening Mr. Truman." General Roger Ramey overlooked the massive amount of debris being brought into the hanger including occupied body bags.

"Classification Falcon Sweep is signed General!" General Ramey physically felt the affliction of Truman's directness, as his tone surged through the phone line. "Concealment is your foremost mission! There's know room for error! Disinformation and concealment agents have been mobilized to piggyback the ruse that has already been established and you are to carry out your orders under the umbrella; is that clear?"

"Yes Mr. President!"

"At this time neither our security sections nor members of my cabinet from the Vice President on down will be privy to this discovery—"

"Oh my God!" The General shouted, cutting the president off.

While heading downstairs to take a closer look at the debris, he suddenly gasped for air as he witnessed three humanoid like creatures being led into the hanger—twelve soldiers with guns trained upon them.

"What is it General?"

"Mr. President, contact has been made. We have living Alien subjects in our possession."

~ ~ ~

The President leaned back in his chair as he was momentarily out of breath—his eyes wild. He then proceeds to call for a staffer using the emergency line.

The staffer quickly made his way into the room, a since of urgency in his tone, "What is it Mr. President?"

"Ready Air Force One!"

"The destination, sir?"

"Roswell, New Mexico!"

The President refocused his attentions back on the General as the staffer quickly left the room to see to the President's order.

"General, no one is to know that I'm en route nor of my arrival."

"Affirmative Mr. President."

~ ~ ~

"Welcome to Roswell, Mr. President. As ordered, we've taken every precaution to shield your visit. You—"

"General, I didn't fly here under the cover of night to have smoke gently blown up my ass. You sent me a pressing telegram shortly after Air Force One took flight reeling on about a message one of the visitors divulged to you. As your telegram omitted the details, I'm sure, because of the sensitivity and needed secrecy— what was the message, General?"

"You have to hear it for yourself, Mr. President."

~ ~ ~

"Mr. President, the other visitors have taken ill and our doctors say that they may be dieing. There's the one before you, here, who seems to be in good health and the one with the message." The General positioned the President at a safe distance from the being. "We've named him EBE short for extraterrestrial biological entity."

EBE curiously took a step towards Truman, staring at the President rather intensely.

Truman felt rather uneasy during this moment of noiselessness and felt the need to speak, "Uh, I'm President Harry S. Truman the premiere representative of the United States of America. I wish—"

"Humanity!"

Without warning the things thoughts suddenly rung in Truman's head as the being seemed unable to speak by way of its mouth. Truman and the General traded a quick glance and instantly the President knew the General heard it too.

"Well, I represent a rather large proportion of our worlds human inhabitants, but if theirs a message you're looking to divulge to our worlds peoples I can assure you, you're speaking to the right person. What is it you're trying to convey?"

"War is upon you!"

Truman stepped rather stealthily closer to the glass enclosure that held the thing and spoke directly, "War!" He shouted. "What do you mean, *war?*"

~ ~ ~

President Truman paced back and forth in the General's office—his features contrite. The General stood at a distance awaiting orders he knew were sure to come, but since it had been more that twenty minutes since they'd left the hanger and the fact that their was a pressing operation underway concerning the incident; he felt the need to speak.

"Mr. President, per your expressed orders on this matter and given the core parameters of Classification Falcon Sweep; I'd be remiss in my duties if I didn't inform you that time is of the essence, sir."

For the first time in nearly half-an-hour, President Truman stopped pacing the floor. "General, you heard what that *thing* said?"

"I did Mr. President."

Truman sighed, "Immediately, you are to gain preliminary Intel from this disclosure with a prime focus on military and technically advanced application. You and you alone will then spearhead the agenda—bringing it to the attention of our National Security Council no later than the 5th of next month with your recommendations. By July 28th I want to receive an outline of your findings so that I may officially brief the NSC on the matter. Be so advised that the power of the presidency will be flanking your every move General; assuring unlimited funding for such a brazen endeavor."

"Mr. President, with what EBE informed us; we're completely outmatched—outgunned in every way," he sighed; "Sir, what it described to us was an invasion!"

"Tell me something I don't know, General?"

"What's the overall objective of this endeavor, Mr. President?"

"Survival!" Truman placed his right hand on the General's shoulder and emphasized his point with his trademark directness, "Humanities survival, General!"

THIS WAS ONLY THE BEGINNING [...]

History is a rather convoluted thing as it is recorded—the sheer weight of the world's words endlessly drowned in a sea of well placed, strategically balanced, yet beautiful lore. As a self-described historian objectivity is a necessity and deathly warranted with such studies, but as an author of questionable fiction who wanders the grandiloquence of history's many gateways; I've always fancied the rim of the steepest literary precipice.

There is no debating the long and unfortunate line of national and international martyrs whose names and actions will forever live on throughout the many pages of world history and through those rare, but inquisitive wild-eyed youths who're truly riveted by the many stories of old; stories that make up only a fraction of humanity's tumultuous history when the truths behind what we believe to be fact are but cleverly disguised mirages.

From my perspective, one of these martyrs happens to have a grand story both in his lifetime and post his untimely demise. One whose overwhelming impact on American history happens to tug at me with such vengeance is our late president John F. Kennedy.

From my exhaustive studies in world history; theirs no question in my mind that history *is* a rather convoluted thing as it is recorded for you see, it all unraveled on the evening of July 3, 1947 in the tiny town of Roswell, New Mexico when a respected business owner Dan Wilmot and his wife were simply relaxing on their front porch. It was on this evening when they witnessed a bright, saucer-shaped object with glowing lights move across the cloudy sky at an undeterminable rate of speed. The next day, a tremendous amount of unearthly debris was discovered in the area. That night proved to be infamous and would later come to be known the world over as the Roswell UFO crash incident.

President Dwight Eisenhower's farewell address to the nation on January 17, 1961 was not only purposeful; it was a cunningly cloaked one so as to not infringe on the presidential oaths or divulge the many secrets he, as all president's, was bound. Eisenhower's address was directly related to the Roswell incident because of what took place in the days that followed. Having succeeded Truman for the Presidency and having read his predecessors notes in the Presidential Book of Secrets; Eisenhower was fully aware of the meeting Truman had with EBE and was in line with Truman's initial precautions given what transpired that evening.

Fully aware of the evolving military trajectory of Classification Falcon Sweep and due to what was surmised of the military and technically advanced Intel that came of their research; Eisenhower watched as this once noble endeavor manifested into a diabolical plot with many thorns. Those thorns were so deeply embedded within the tactical arms divisions of our nation that not even the power of the presidency could stop it.

One thorn was code named the Aneman Project—an unsanctioned experiment aimed at developing a superhuman armed force using the men and women of our armed forces. And so it was that Eisenhower's farewell address to our nation was as prescient as it was bold in its delivery—a targeted warning to all

Americans and the peoples of the world when he stated, "*In the councils of government, we must guard against the acquisition of unwarranted influence, whether sought or unsought, by the military industrial complex.*"

With President Eisenhower's address seeming to fall upon deaf ears; maybe because of the unusual heaviness of his words at that particular time in history, the strategic military experimentations that took place after the Roswell incident existed and persisted without pause and ultimately lead to the November 22, 1963 assassination of President John F. Kennedy. Behind the assassination lay a vast conspiracy well hidden within the complexity of a massive bureaucratic spider web that *we the people* have come to believe and accept when, in fact, Project Aneman was the mainspring of our president's demise.

This is what happened and I know that this will be an extremely hard pill to swallow, but it must be told. Project Aneman reached an evolved testing phase and needed a war. Vietnam was that war. Kennedy was in the way.

Bang!

Bang!

Jim Marrs, author of the critically acclaimed book Crossfire, published in 1989 made one of the most important statements ever written concerning the assassination of President John F. Kennedy, which I believe you should take into consideration when it comes to my story: "*Do not trust this book. In fact, when it comes to the assassination of President John F. Kennedy don't trust any one source or even the basic evidence and testimony. In the case of the JFK assassination, belief and trust have long been a part of the problem.*"

As a pragmatic author of fact-based fiction and in order to protect my life and the lives of my family—I present the totality of what I've discovered not only through the covert council of my anonymous source and an extremely rigorous research process, but in a fashion that demonstrates the unfettered draw of Speculative

Fiction. Simply put, I present my story as a warning wrapped in a lie in order to tell you the truth.

Mark Twain may have been writing about this very project of mine when he wrote that truth is stranger than fiction, because "fiction is obliged to stick to possibilities; *truth* isn't."

A.K. Kuykendall
Author

Prologue

Rocky Mountain National Park and Roosevelt National Forest surround the village of Estes Park, Colorado, with spectacular mountain scenery, wildlife, miles of hiking trails, and scenic drives. Within this beautiful country, the scenic Trail Ridge Road travels over the Continental Divide.

People have long visited this valley to enjoy beautiful mountain scenery, its moderate climate, and abundant wildlife. During an unusual cold spell, I sit here atop the glacial rock known as Sharktooth. I sit with my Medal of Honor in my palm, my eyes fixed on nothing and everything at once on this December afternoon. I sit upon American soil, as across the nation, Americans stage an all-out revolt. "Americans against America" is written in the headlines of every major newspaper and spouted by news broadcasters from here to the Earth's edge.

I feel a little bit closer to heaven, here on Sharktooth. And so I let my thoughts wander, for I feel the need to escape the upheaval of my country here in the land of the soaring eagle.

A heavy fist has fallen upon Americans with the rule of big government. Martial law runs amok in the fifty states and our government steadily tightens the noose. They've now tied the hands of American citizens who rebel against authority.

On Tuesday, March 25, 2012, Americans succumbed to entrapment, beginning the slow-but-certain rise of a governmental superpower and the separation from what we held true: America, land of the once free—home of the once brave.

Once they knew the truth, Americans began an uprising never seen before, including Democrats, Republicans, the religious, the not-so-religious, the poor, the rich, the young, the old, the dying, and the enlisted. Together they rebelled against a government that had come to base its evolution on deception, corruption, and death.

Northern Colorado dims in reality as the continued evolution of the Rocky Mountains falls heavy over the land itself. Glacial erosion is an ongoing process lasting hundreds of thousands of years. I sit here with a sharp realization: the world is changing drastically.

This particular December day offers me a desperately needed vacation. Here in the heart of the Rocky Mountains, the land seems peaceful, with snow-peaked mountains as far as the eye can see. It's amazing to think these huge peaks were formed by glaciers, and I can't help thinking—if our climate cools, the summers will no longer be warm enough to melt the winter snow.

Amazing!

Glaciers form when snow accumulates, compacts under its own weight, and forms an icy block. They are commonly a thousand feet thick—often thicker in places. I sit at the peak of this mountain because I desire to witness, however slowly, the marvel of a glacier flowing downhill.

As a glacier moves, it picks up loose boulders and carries them. These boulders scour the underlying rock, grinding away like sandpaper on wood. After thousands of years, gorges are carved out and the glacier carries away the rocks, called tills when carried by the icy mountain.

Behind the glaciers, wilderness flourishes and life seems to return to a time when the land was wild and corruption wasn't even a word; a time when men and women praised the spirits and lived free, before Europeans set foot on foreign land, arriving on huge floating vessels the Indians referred to as winged canoes of the gods. These white-fleshed strangers were greeted with hospitality tempered with understandable caution by the warriors. In time, the Indian people were punished for their kindness, judged as weak by those same strangers. They were butchered by the tens of thousands and stripped of the land they had never proclaimed to be theirs in the first place. The Indian people lived close to their gods and the land that fed, housed, bathed and loved them. They never took its gifts for granted. But these foreigners from foreign lands didn't share or respect their beliefs.

America began its evolution long ago, when Columbus boldly claimed the country for his queen. Although the new land was already inhabited, Europeans felt the Indian people were a minor hurdle—a wild race who wore damn near nothing, spoke a language never heard before and lived in pristine peace, free of detrimental politics. Theirs was a race that felt no need to compete for a living and lived off the very land they walked upon.

They prayed to their environment, not a Christian god, and the Europeans thought of them as savage blasphemers. Surely they did not deserve the vast land upon which they had built their lives. Here in the mountains, my surroundings make me think of the unflattering development of our country.

And so I sit, after a bracing free climb which took me high above Andrews Tarn's rushing streams of melted snow and deep blue sparkling water. I sit, quiet and alone, with one ear to the frosted wind and a simmering, vindictive smile upon my face, for I played an essential role in the revolution.

My cabin is nestled on a hillside behind me, only sixteen yards from the lake, and there I find some measure of peace. I can smell the hickory that burns in my fireplace, and the white smoke rising from my chimney catches the wind and elevates to higher altitudes.

My life is a twisted riddle. The deadly blue haze I see in the eastern sky is fast approaching. But I relax, because the environment won't affect me here; brisk winds from the snow-peaked mountains will protect me.

Just a few years ago, I never would have guessed that I would soon be able to lift a boulder weighing more than six hundred thirty pounds, yet today I can elevate this boulder and—with the slightest jerk of my brachioradialis, forearm flexors, and the brachialis—toss the solid mass forty feet without so much as a second thought.

I'd like to say I'm one of those comic book heroines like Super Girl, Hawk Woman, or Wonder Woman, that I'm some sort of anomaly born with mutant DNA. I'd love to claim that there are more like me out there, all fighting for a place in this world among the human race. And sure, an explanation would be easier if I were an extraterrestrial sent from Krypton, that the yellow sun of the planet Earth boosts my natural strength and prevents me from harm.

I wish any of that were true, but the fact of the matter is, my body and strength is simply a product of humanity's insane drive for absolute power over our own species.

The marvelous transition I underwent that day reinvented me as a new subspecies of humanity. In about an hour and a half, this American pawn was promoted to the rank of a royal guardian.

As I sit here staring into the dark blue haze from my safe place, I find peace in my evolution. My life was never easy; born and raised in the tiny town of Macon, Mississippi, I was a child of abuse—physical, sexual, and mental— growing up in a whirlwind that would define my whole existence. To cope with my past, I became an overachiever. Everything I touched seemed to glow like a rising rocket. With every achievement, I pushed my soiled history further behind me. I felt that if I continuously pushed on, never stopping for breath, I wouldn't have time to think about the past. This kept me from the adolescent breakdown I feared was always near. My abused past kept me from ever wanting the company of a man, love, or friendship; this deep-rooted phobia formed in me as an introspective personality with a rough exterior.

My life is defined by pride and regret, but one thing is certain: as a little girl in Macon, I never could have imagined the life I would lead. The Army is my home, my life, my destiny, and ultimately my reason for living. Without the Corps, I would have become a career criminal before my seventeenth birthday. I already had a juvenile record boasting eight counts of petty theft and sixteen counts of assault. I was what you'd call a troubled youth, which is how society often labels young adults who are trying to find their place in this world.

After the murder-suicide of my mother and father, I was left to fend for my five-year-old baby brother, Reggie. My life changed instantly when that responsibility fell onto my shoulders. Although I looked after my brother through his tantrums and trials, I remained psychologically distant from him. He understood, because we shared the same history. His eyes served as silent witnesses to my pain again and again.

When our parents were still alive, our house doubled as a medieval torture dungeon. On my seventh birthday I was hiding from my father in the basement of that dungeon when I found a scrap of a poem stuffed under a pile of exercise equipment. I held onto that poem with as much nurturing love as I would hold a nurturing parent, one who'd wake me up on Saturday morning for buttermilk pancakes, sausage links, maple syrup heated with a swirl of fresh butter, and a special pancake for Reggie shaped like Mickey Mouse.

The journey of love:
as mysterious to the human
as the world can be
to the seeking scientist.
Destiny, a phenomenon
pondered for centuries!
Though no one knows,
the hope of it lies within; as
Love is that mysterious entity
which destiny holds near.

I wish this was a love story. Instead, this is a story of conspiracies taken to the extreme, focusing on the inner core of our very own government. Collectively, every one of us are nothing but pieces in a domestic, foreign, and most assuredly intergalactic chess game. We are mere pawns, continually sacrificed at the whim of players with God complexes. The terms "democracy" and "freedom" are concepts forged from a common fairytale. In this story, we're a pack of conditioned sheep running aimlessly about—fooling ourselves into believing in our own freedom. We're nothing but eating, pissing, shitting, procreating, overworked, taxpaying, childlike creatures soaring the skies of Neverland, the pixie dust nothing more than a strategic concentration of pure bullshit.

The ignorance of my fellow Americans shocks me every time I encounter it. How could one really believe in a society's infallibility, as if we could achieve our superpower status without corruption? We're living proof that our so-called freedom is truly a trumped-up lie.

This story circles my life as a highly trained Special Forces team leader within the Army Rangers—the kick-ass 4th Battalion, 76th Ranger Regiment, to be exact. Throughout my years in the Corps, I never could have imagined what was possible within the Armed Forces that defend the United States and its supposed freedoms. Little did I know, I had dedicated my life to defending individual interests.

And that's not just America: every humanoid is enslaved from birth. We're slaves controlled by our own materialistic wants, conditioned not to notice the cunning, secretive nature of the players. Whether it's the National Security Agency, the Central Intelligence Agency, the Federal Bureau of Investigation, or the Secret Service, corruption seeps from every angle of the government.

Allow me to introduce myself further: I'm Major Kalista Flaker of the United States Army. To this day, my life has been a constant battle climbing steep and unforgiving stone. You might think that this chapter of my life began in January 2004, when I was promoted from Captain to Major, and subsequently reassigned back into the fold of the Special Forces unit known as the Army Rangers. Or, you might place the beginning of this story seventeen years ago, the morning I discovered chicanery within the boundaries of our National Security Agency. In fact, this story's root stretches back to 1947.

Part I

The Fortified Shroud

Conspirator's Odyssey

Dan Wilmot and his wife sat on their front porch admiring a fast-approaching storm. Thick dark clouds rippled the night sky and flashes of lightning brightened the fields.

In the middle of the spectacular light show, a long streak of lightning ripped through the sky. Dan and his wife sat up in alarm as six seconds of daylight illuminated the town before the lightning vanished as quickly as it had arrived. They heard a cracking noise from above, sounding exactly like a firecracker had been set off near the house. Then, they saw a bright, saucer-shaped object move across the sky, its lights glowing.

* * *

Mac Brazel, foreman of the J. B. Foster Ranch, rode his horse out to check the sheep after a night of intense storms. While he was there, he discovered a large amount of strange debris scattered across one of the ranch pastures.

"What in the hell," the old foreman said to himself.

Spooked by the debris, Mac's horse began galloping back and forth, turning violently around, and leaping into the air. With the horse finally calmed, Mac gathered pieces of the debris to carry home with him. The next morning, he called George Wilcox.

* * *

The silence of the empty sheriff's station was cut by a ringing telephone. Sheriff Wilcox ran from the bathroom to answer the call. "Sheriff's office—this is Wilcox."

"George, it's Mac Brazel. Look here, I found some stuff out on the ranch that's really thrown me for a loop—"

Sheriff Wilcox looked around his empty office. "I'm a little shorthanded today, Mac. What is it that's got you spooked?"

"My horse is spooked, Sheriff; I'm more amazed than anything. I showed it to a couple of close friends of mine before I called and they can't figure it out, either. If you don't mind, I'd like you to see it for yourself."

"If you're not being robbed or chased by a knife-wielding madman, I'm sorry to say I'm not leaving this office."

"I'm on my way to town to pick up some supplies anyway. I'll just stop by, if that's all right with you."

The sheriff sighed. "All right, Mac," he said. "See you later."

Within the hour, Mac came bursting through the main door of the sheriff's station clutching a large, dirty rag that carried some of the ranch site debris. Anxious to find answers, Mac had left the engine running in his old Chevy pickup, which he had double-parked beside Sheriff Wilcox's mud-coated police cruiser. He held the rag in one fist while dinging the counter bell with the other.

"Hold your horses," Wilcox said, making his way around the corner to see Mac Brazel breathing heavy, beads of sweat on his brow.

Wilcox glanced at his watch. "Damn, Mac! You run a footrace?"

"Take a look for yourself," Mac said, placing the rag on the counter with the same care he would give a newborn.

Looking out the front window, Wilcox saw Mac's double-parked pickup and removed the toothpick from out of his mouth. "I knew you were one of those fancy UT scholarship boys," he said, "but I didn't realize you were above the law in my town."

"George, since you got elected sheriff, you've turned into a real asshole." Mac slid the rag over to Wilcox. "Just take a look at this stuff. I've got better things to do than fight you all day." He turned and left, slamming the door behind him.

"Look here, you called on me, not the other way around!" Wilcox shouted out the window as Mac returned to his truck.

"In that case, do your damn job!" Mac called back.

Placing the toothpick back in his mouth, Wilcox snatched the rag and its contents off the counter and headed for his office. Halfway there, something fell out of the satchel and hit the floor, sending a hollow metallic sound bouncing off the walls for about ten to fifteen seconds. Wilcox had never heard a sound like that before. Bending down he saw the culprit was a flat seven-inch piece of metal no wider than a fingernail file. It weighed about as much as a standard envelope. It wasn't clear how such a small object could make so much noise. Picking it up hesitantly, the sheriff took a seat behind his desk.

Wilcox placed the object on his desk and unwrapped the rest of the material to find two more objects. One was a solid, foot-long piece that resembled a dull hook. Strange markings looped around the entire curved material but when he touched it, the markings vanished, only to reappear when he let go. The last item resembled a smooth piece of aluminum: two feet long, a foot wide, and less than an inch thick. The panel was incredibly light and felt like a cushioned slab of marble. He could fold and unfold this piece, and found that it didn't become wrinkled, dented, or creased.

The sheriff leaned back in his chair and studied a fighter pilot poster tacked to his wall—a typical marketing gesture care of the Roswell Army Air Base. He picked up his phone and dialed the number listed at the bottom of the poster.

* * *

Major Jesse Marcel, intelligence officer for the 509th Bomb Group, was involved in recovering the Roswell wreckage. A team of fifty soldiers gathered the debris into trucks and transported it out of sight and onto the Roswell Army Air Field.

Acting as spokesperson, Major Marcel briefly answered questions for a group of reporters gathered outside the blockade. "The aforementioned wreckage that I'm sure you've heard about by now no longer resides in New Mexico. At this time, it's not clear as to what the wreckage is compiled of or where it came from. Thank you, that's all."

As he spoke, a dozen trucks behind him moved out, leaving the entourage of reporters shuffling on the pavement.

* * *

The headline story of the *Roswell Daily Record* revealed that the wreckage of a flying saucer had been recovered from a ranch in the area. When questioned, Major Marcel disclosed the wreckage was flown from New Mexico on to higher headquarters. Colonel William Blanchard, commander of the 509th Bomb Group, issued a press release stating the wreckage of a crashed disk had been recovered.

A second press release was issued from the office of General Roger Ramey, commander of the Eighth Air Force at Fort Worth Army Airfield, within hours of the first. The second statement rescinded the first and claimed officers of the 509th Bomb Group had incorrectly identified a weather balloon and its radar reflector as a crashed disk.

* * *

In the *Daily Record* office, reporters scrambled to make print in light of the new information. The lead reporter, Jeff Begals, spoke to his fellow reporters.

"The shit's going to hit the fan!" he said. "These military boys aren't covering this one up. We need to get an ear to the Pentagon—to the White House, for that matter. I'd bet my last nickel those Washington boys are fully aware of what happened here in Roswell. They're slipping! What is it, a flying disk, weather balloon, what? The stories don't make sense because they're lying! I know they're lying to us."

"Jeff, goddammit, that's nothing new," said Todd Richards, the newsroom's chief.

"But this is a big deal," Begals persisted. "You know how these boys operate better than any of us. I'm going to yank out the truth. After this, that Pulitzer won't pass me by again."

Richards tried to stare Begals down, but finally waved to the group. "All right, you lowlife losers. Let's get a goddamn ear to the Pentagon and the White House. See if there's any chatter. Get me a goddamn story to print. Now move, move, move, move—"

* * *

The Ballard Funeral Home in Roswell had a contract to provide ambulance and mortuary services for the Roswell Army Air Field. Glenn Dennis was a young mortician at Ballard and one of Begals's contacts. Dennis had received several telephone calls from the mortuary officer at the airfield before the wreckage was recovered. The officer had asked about using small, hermetically sealed caskets and requested a recommendation on preserving bodies that had been exposed to the elements for several days.

His curiosity piqued, Dennis visited the base hospital that evening, but was forcibly escorted from the building. This behavior only incited his curiosity, so he arranged to meet a nurse from the base hospital in a coffee shop the next day.

"So, tell me, what was the big secret at the hospital last night?" Dennis asked, sipping his coffee. "They practically threw me out on my ear."

The pretty young nurse lit a cigarette with trembling hands. She looked over her shoulder before leaning in. "They brought in small, non-human bodies," she whispered urgently. She told Dennis she'd attended the autopsies performed on these creatures. As she spoke, she sketched what she'd seen on a napkin. Dennis kept the drawing.

This meeting was to be their last, and Glenn Dennis could learn no more about the alien bodies. The nurse was abruptly transferred to England within the next few days.

* * *

National Security Council - August 5, 1947

General Roger Ramey stepped up onto a well-lit podium equipped with a microphone and began to speak:

"Gentlemen, forty thousand years of evolution and we've barely scratched the vastness of human potential. Until today, that is. We have found that the extraterrestrial bodies and their unique infrastructure, metabolism, and regenerative characteristics may be of great use to the United States, given the time and resources for further research."

"What is it you want from us, General?" a voice echoed from the shadows.

"The items we collected at the crash site need to be broken down and analyzed for future military use. Given what we've already learned, we have the potential to create soldiers who will perform in the field like nothing the world has ever seen."

* * *

The White House - November 22, 1963

Pages and assistants moved around him in all directions as President Kennedy prepared for his trip to Dallas.

At the start of this day, the president took time in his already hectic schedule to call a secret meeting of his counsel. Eight men, including Vice President Lyndon B. Johnson, sat in the Oval Office, watching their leader pace the room. Kennedy addressed the men:

"Now, gentlemen, the Vietnamese council stands strong in their convictions. I don't want an all-out war."

The men glanced at one another.

"It's crazy to sacrifice the lives of our boys," Kennedy said. "This is a new era. Diplomacy will be our initial weapon, and so help me God, war is our last resort." He picked up the war decree from his desk. "These documents will be filed indefinitely. Furthermore, I will order our troops out of Vietnam, effective noon on November 25, 1963. I ask you to bear with me as we show the world a different side of our great nation."

Minutes after the meeting, a White House representative handed the president's executive chef a capsule filled with an ashy white substance, accompanied by a note. The paper read: *IT'S A GO.* The chef held the note in his gas burner, letting it crinkle into ashes. He finished making the president's breakfast, using the foreign powder in his recipe.

* * *

As Kennedy finished breakfast, an aide entered the room to inform him it was time to go.

Standing, Kennedy brushed himself off. "Gurdi?" he said with a smile.

"Yes, Mr. President?"

"I tell you, I love people with everything I'm worth, and as strange as this may sound, I also fear them."

"Why is that, Mr. President?"

"People are what bring people down."

Gurdi smiled. She stood nearby as Kennedy, always the hopeless romantic, pulled a rose from a nearby bouquet to present to his wife in the car.

* * *

Air Force One - November 22, 1963

Lyndon B. Johnson and the seven other men who sat in the Oval Office earlier that morning gathered in a private room on Air Force One, watching Kennedy's assassination on television. The men laughed quietly to themselves, exchanging handshakes and nods.

Johnson signed the war decree with a flourish. "You men did your part and made me your thirty-sixth president. Now I'll do my part and show those gook Vietcong bastards what we're made of. Compromise isn't in those yellow monkeys' vocabulary. I strongly believe what you boys are working on will make history and ultimately strengthen our nation. Fuck that Irish nigger-loving JFK and his so-called vision! He was soft on Communism and he ate a bullet for his weakness. The United States of America is a superpower, and so help me God, we will remain that way."

* * *

TOTAL AMERICAN CASUALTIES IN NON-COMBAT INCIDENTS: **18,786**
TOTAL NUMBER OF VIETNAMESE CIVILIAN CASUALTIES: **20,884**
CAUSE OF CASUALTIES: **AMERICAN SOLDIERS**
PROBABLE REASONING FOR THESE CASUALTIES: **INSANITY**
CAUSE OF INSANITY: **CLASSIFIED**

* * *

Vietnam - August 5, 1966

The Sai Lau camp was a sanctuary for Vietnamese civilians caught in the battlefield. There, they escaped the scene of war, but not the sounds. Every day, explosive air raids in the distance dropped 27 metric-ton bombs, each run flown by three B-52s in V-formation. Such a trio could easily drop ninety tons of arsenal at once. The stutter of AK-47 and rifle gunfire rang through the air, and screams bounced off the trees. The sounds echoed for miles.

Most raids were launched from Guam. The flight of passing Russian-provided Vietnamese MIGs and American F-105 Thunderchief fighters filled the skies.

Misty dew concentrated with napalm and pistol dust blanketed everything. Bullets, grenades, and an array of air strikes manicured the brush as though an unorthodox landscaper was using American and Vietcong solders as his bulldozer and crew.

The ambushes rained blood from the sky as shrapnel chewed men to pieces. Camps filled with Americans waiting to begin or re-enter a tour of duty. Entire teams would disappear into the jungle, most never to return. Civilians hid in the jungle, as only the wealthy were able to flee before American and Vietcong troops ravaged the land. Eighty percent of the Vietnamese population lived in the war zone.

Hollow reverberations shook the ground in the Sai Lau camp. Twelve Marines holding M-16s emerged cautiously from a bushy swamp. Their gun muzzles were protected by condoms, for the weapons proved unreliable when wet—a definite drawback in this jungle war. Soldiers were often found dead beside their dismantled weapons, killed while attempting a quick repair.

The Marines stood quietly at the jungle's edge, watching a village filled with women, children, and elderly. Eight Vietcong soldiers rampaged through the village, cursing and screaming at old men before cutting off their heads.

A few Vietcong pulled ladies and little girls up and took them into the huts; horrific screams emerged. The soldiers outside laughed at the sound. Two of the camp's boys were thrown onto their knees, handed knives by Vietcong soldiers, and forced to cut at each other.

Captain Rufus Innius was a rough-looking white boy from Brooklyn who had been on tour since the initial all-out deployment in 1963. In his latest stint, he served as platoon leader of the men watching from the bushes. He signaled for his men to circle the camp.

Two of the American soldiers rushed in and quietly eliminated the two Vietcong who were making the boys cut each other. Other members of the team rushed into the huts, killing the remaining guerillas. Captain Innius carried out fourteen-year-old Su Lee, severely beaten and badly bleeding from her inner thighs.

"Doc, get over here!" Captain Innius shouted. He put Su Lee down gently in the clearing and stood back. "Men, secure this camp," he said, hiding his tears. "I don't want the smell of lizard piss breaching our perimeter—you got that?"

The men rushed off to follow the captain's orders. The medic, Sergeant Major Dick Gregore, rushed in and began tending to the girl.

As he observed the scene, Captain Innius heard a noise from one of the huts. He pulled his sidearm and approached. Inside, he found Private Vic Moones, a skinny 21-year-old white Mississippi-born country boy, fully naked and curled up in a corner. Moones was sweating. The clothing lying around him seemed ripped directly from his body.

Captain Innius crouched down. "Moones, what the fuck are you doing?" he asked, trying not to shout. He figured the man had cracked under pressure.

"I can't say. I mean, I don't know. You have to tell me, because I don't know!" Moones squirmed on the floor, his eyes wild.

"Stand up, soldier."

"Quiet! You're hurting my ears, man." Captain Innius stood, balled his fists and stepped toward the insubordinate private. Moones jolted back as if his captain's step was as loud as an exploding mine.

"Boy I'm gonna crack your skull," Captain Innius said. "Remember your protocol, Private. I'm not one of your buddies in hokey-poke Mississippi; you refer to me as Sir. Got that?"

Moones wept, his whole body shaking. "The noise—"

Captain Innius pulled Moones to his feet, drawing his pistol with his free hand. Moones grabbed the officer's gun and broke it in half, his bare hands twisting the metal. Before Innius could respond, Moones lifted him into the air with one hand and tossed him through the wall of the hut.

The young captain barely had time to find his ass under him before Moones followed him out, clutching his head. "The noise!" he screeched. Soldiers ran from all corners of the village.

"Shoot him!" Captain Innius called out to them.

"Cap, it's Moones!" said one of his men.

Moones advanced on them, screaming. "Shoot him—that's a direct order! Put him down!"

First Lieutenant Banes hesitated for only a moment before firing two shots into Moones's chest, knocking him to the ground.

For a moment, everyone became quiet. A few of the men turned to Banes, glaring at him, beginning to approach.

Captain Innius rolled to his feet, walked to the body of his man Moones and bent down to check for a pulse. Getting nothing, he rose and confronted his men.

"You will follow the orders of your commanding officer!" he shouted with the same tone he had used back in Basic. The men straightened up, confused. "I do the thinking in this squad! Every order I give is taken as law! Do I make myself clear?"

Before any man could respond, Private Moones leapt to his feet and attacked Captain Innius, ripping his body apart like he was tearing a single sheet of tissue paper.

The men rushed into the shocking fray and Moones killed them two at a time. Screams and gunfire rang through the village as Moones crushed his comrades with his bare hands, his eyes wild.

Su Lee, the girl who had just had her life saved by the American men dying before her, witnessed all of it. She saw Moones stagger out of camp before she passed out and was found unconscious by a convoy of American soldiers about four hours later.

* * *

She woke up in an American hospital in Saigon surrounded by dozens of soldiers. The shock of seeing the curious men sent her back into deep unconsciousness.

While she was out, an American squadron spotted friendly walking in a minefield. The American was naked, bleeding from his chest, and seemingly unaware of his surroundings.

Captain Jeremy Gordin signaled his squadron to quiet. "People," he hissed, "Whatever's he's on, it killed him way before he stepped onto that field."

Private Moones stepped on a landmine. Flesh and bone scattered across the field, material that would be trampled over by other soldiers as the war raged on. But a ghost would roam those killing fields forever.

"What in the fuck is happening to these soldiers," Captain Gordin said to himself. He pulled out a rolled cigarette, lit it, and took a few drags, watching the field.

* * *

New York City - February 26, 1993

The Twin Towers stood as dual witnesses to the lunch hour, the overhead sun turning its windows golden. Sixteen National Security Agency agents, dressed in black suits and sunglasses, huddled in a well-hidden lab below the parking garage.

One researcher handed a black case over to Agent Damion Walker. Walker and his team boarded a five-Hummer caravan, and drove from the towers.

"Make it happen," Walker said into a secured communicator.

"Okay, listen up." Agent Doug Ingro looked at his wristwatch. "Time is 12:17. In fifty-two seconds, you are to detonate. I repeat: you are to detonate."

Moments later, a blinding flash of light glittered in the rearview mirrors.

2

The deadly war in Vietnam had come and gone. The killing fields lay still from sunup, through the hot October day, through the pale orange sunsets. Vietnamese typically avoid the eerie plains out of respect to the men, women, and children who met their fate there.

Across those quiet Vietnamese plains, a team of twenty-two soldiers ran in dedicated file. Captain Kalista Flaker brought up the rear perimeter, a lookout for trouble.

Flaker stopped for a moment, lifting her binoculars to note a series of ruffles in the bushes off to the right. She analyzed the movement for just a few moments before calling for her team—

3

On a night where wind meets the fury of dark clouds on a soggy November dusk, scorpions give birth to a new breed. Distant mountain craters resemble Nepal, the Gurkhas' mountain kingdom. Hidden beneath the soil are ages of prehistoric bone and decay. Above ground, reptilian predators hunt for food. Eighteen miles east of Las Vegas stands the remote community of Dingostone—dotted with hometown gas stations, mom-and-pop restaurants, community theaters, and military housing. Thirty miles west of town stands one of the largest army bases in the United States: Post Base 22-987 Dingo, formerly known as Area S-4. This base was once believed to be in Papoose Lake, south of Groom Lake—the infamous Area 51.

Dingostone is a direct extension of Kingman, Arizona, approximately 150 miles southeast of Las Vegas. Post Base 22-987 Dingo was said to have a surface base in Dingostone, plus an underground tunnel system that stretched the full 150 miles to Kingman.

After the first clap of thunder roared through the town, rain damped the pavement outside the main gate. Two white-walled, black-trimmed guardposts sat on opposite sides of the rocky road. Inside the posts, two drenched MPs stood guard, rifles in hand. Two more MPs stood just outside, facing each other, standing under an extended shower guard.

Three pearl-black Hummers with tinted windows blazed through the streets, rocking over bumps in the road and kicking up mud. As they approached the guards, the Hummers came to a quick halt and a window lowered in the lead vehicle.

The driver passed the guard a yellow laminated card centered with a large black dot, and then quickly closed the window. Within seconds, the card evaporated in the MP's hand, causing him and the other guards to look at each other and swiftly about-face.

The two gate guards hustled with the gates. Clearly, these Hummers were the vessels of Special Ops royalty.

* * *

Dim lighting engulfed the room. It was dark enough already, with rain beating against the windows. Lightning flared outside. Twelve coarse-faced men, age 40 and up, stood in General George Thimpkin's office. Each man wore identical black tailored suits. Thimpkin sat at his desk, dignified in his uniform. His hair carried streaks of gray but he was in good shape for his age, with patient eyes and the overall look of an experienced, confident leader. One of the men stepped up to his desk.

"Sir, the wire will come soon, and that will only set us back."

"Our cover is our most important objective, agent," said Thimpkin, tapping his fingers on the desk. He hesitated, staring out the window. "Fine," he said. "Send a team—"

A secretary's voice came over the speakerphone. "General, I'm sorry for disturbing you, but there's a call from the White House. It's the Vice President, sir."

Thimpkin extracted a cigar from his top desk drawer and lit it. The men in the room stared at each other while he took a long drag.

Thimpkin reached over to the phone. "Thanks, Gail. Patch him through."

He took another thoughtful drag before putting the phone to his ear. "Gore, you dodging son of a bitch, I haven't heard from you in a while. You and William lucked out and held onto your jobs, and you go and miss my annual fly-fishing invitational. I'll tell you right now, I didn't vote for either one of your asses." Smiling, Thimpkin leaned back in his chair. "To what do I owe the pleasure?" His facial expression changed almost immediately. "Yes, sir. I'll be there. Of course. Soon."

He looked at the phone and put it down. With a sigh, he tucked his cigar into his mouth, placed his elbows on the desk and intertwined his fingertips.

"Well, gentlemen, that was the wire."

A man near the back of the room spoke up. "What's the plan, sir?"

"I'm going to handpick the team," Thimpkin said. "It will be headed by one of my strongest officers—Captain Kalista Flaker. She's platoon leader of one of my best Ranger groups, the 4th Battalion, 76th Ranger Regiment."

If any of the men had heard of her, they did not make their knowledge known.

"Are you aware of the Best Ranger Competition?" Thimpkin asked. "It's an annual event conducted by the RTB in honor of a good friend and colleague of mine, David Grange, director of the Ranger Department and Fort Benning's post commander. The goal is to determine the best two-man buddy team in the Rangers. It's a three-day event, physical and mental tasks, little rest, the whole thing. The attrition rate averages sixty percent. I've won it eight times. I was the guest speaker in 1989, when Captain Flaker, a first-timer, proved a force. She and her wingman, First Lieutenant Frank Cassio—they call him Ghost—they came within inches of winning. She was devastated when someone else took the honors ahead of her." He walked to his office window and peered out into the rain-soaked courtyard. "That's the only time I've known Captain Flaker to fail at anything."

Outside in the courtyard, eleven rugged soldiers, nine men and two women, gripped ropes bare-handed, blinking against the rain. The ropes were connected to a sturdy log the size of a telephone pole with a walking platform at the top and ladders on either side. The structure stood sixty feet tall and the ropes dangled twenty feet below that—the only way down or up was a difficult climb. On the ground level was a deep, muddy pool. This endurance test was a regular choice of troop leaders.

One by one, everyone dropped, leaving Captain Flaker dangling alone. Once the last solder fell, she put one hand over the other, climbing while the other men and women splashed down and swam out. At the top she rang a cowbell, lifted herself to the platform, and gave a brisk wave to her regiment below. They cheered her for yet another victory.

After he saw her effort at the ranger competition, General Thimpkin had sent Flaker overseas to train in France with one of the world's most grueling training regiments, France's 1st Parachute Regiment, Marine Infantry. This regiment was part of the 11th Parachute Division, similar to the old British Five Airborne Brigades. It had two brigades, with seven battalions below them, called regiments by the French. The Parachute Regiment and the 1st Parachute Regiment, Marine Infantry were the most outstanding groups. Although the other regiments reported to their brigades, the 1st Parachute Regiment, Marine Infantry reported directly to the 11th Parachute Division and had a stronger Special Forces role than other regiments. It was actually descended from the SAS units set up in France during WWII to help the British SAS fight the

Nazis. The 1st Parachute Regiment, Marine Infantry developed into France's elite Special Operations unit, tasked with counterterrorism and hostage rescue missions both inside and outside France. Other tasks included body guarding, reconnaissance, sabotage, and unconventional warfare. Elements of the division had been deployed to Bosnia, Kosovo, Chad, Lebanon, and other hot spots. They were the best of the best; the perfect place for a promising young soldier.

Still sitting atop the wooden structure, Flaker spotted Thimpkin watching her and gave him a jaunty salute. He returned it with a half-salute and turned back to the men in his office.

"Yes, Captain Flaker will lead our team."

* * *

Macon, Mississippi - Thirty Years Earlier

Young Kalista Flaker sat at the kitchen table of the kind of shack that barely offered adequate shelter to cockroaches. Kalista was five years old and skinny, with large, hungry eyes.

Her mother, an overweight drunk, slammed a doll down onto the table in front of the girl. "You little bitch," the woman slurred. "I told you to have your room clean before I got home. Get your ass in your room and stay there! I'm going to tell your Daddy about this when he gets home."

Kalista pulled her doll off the table, cradling it in her arms. "Please don't tell Daddy," she said. "I'll clean it up, I promise."

Her mother reached across the table and slapped her, a mouth-numbing slap that set her ears ringing.

Kalista, her lip seeping blood, stared up at her mother.

The woman took a long drink from her plastic cup. "Get your ass in your room now, goddammit!"

Kalista ran, crying.

* * *

28

Nicaragua - 1985

An intense daydream set Captain Flaker's heart racing. She reoriented herself: she was sitting in a foxhole, in an imbedded ranger regiment in support of the Contras, holding her assault weapon close to her face.

Ghost sat beside her, seemingly asleep. When an enemy grenade sailed over their heads and landed in the pit, he moved in a smooth single motion, tossing the grenade back out and hitting the deck with her. Sounds of explosions and gunfire rang through the night air.

4

The city glowed on a beautiful sunny afternoon in February, with traffic bustling through the downtown streets, horns and sirens echoing off the tall buildings. Lieutenant Riondro Buckner and his family—wife Sharon, sons Trent and Bobby, aged seven and nine—were bound for the park.

Riondro, a dashing nine-year veteran of the Navy with a promising future in the Corps, loved spending time with his family. He was only four days away from rising to the status of a Gannet in the SEALS, and he knew it wouldn't be easy. But this had been his personal objective from the first day of his enlistment and he had moved steadily up the ranks without a hitch so far.

Even his daydreams in the past few weeks had been focused on the SEAL team. Riondro smiled to himself, the smile of a man who had worked his whole life to become a part of a premier naval special operations force, proficient in not only underwater ops and demolitions, but also reconnaissance and small-unit tactics.

Bobby snapped him out of his reverie. "Are we there yet?"

"I'm hungry," Trent said.

Sharon laughed, surprised that they had remained quiet for as long as they did. "Be quiet and let your dad study," she said, glancing in the rearview mirror.

"Dad's not in school! He doesn't have to study," Bobby said.

Riondro glanced at his wife. "Have I been ignoring you too long?"

"It's all right, sweetheart. This one's a big deal. You'd better be prepared for my test."

"What test?"

She shushed him. "Later," she said. "The kids are being quiet for you."

Riondro took advantage of the silence to daydream as they drove. SEAL training was an arduous affair that lasted six months and included the infamous Hell Week. Once he passed the training, he would have a six-month probation period before he could pin on the golden Budweiser.

He found a meter by Central Park. The whole family hauled their gear and set up camp under an old oak tree. As Sharon made plates for the boys and herself, Riondro chipped a bag of ice into manageable chunks.

He filled their drinks with ice and took a seat next to his wife. "Sharon, may I have something to eat please?"

"First things first, are you ready?"

"Ready for what?" Riondro noticed the boys were giggling, their mouths full of fried chicken.

"Your test," Sharon said, smiling. "I've let you go over everything while we've been driving, so here is your test. What are the three categories used to separate your gear?"

"How—?"

"I've been reading, so you have to answer before you get your meal." She loaded up a plate of chicken and held it just out of his reach.

"Yes, ma'am," Riondro said. "First-line gear includes everyday essentials needed for survival. Battle dress uniforms, weapons, maps, compasses, and watches are all first-line gear. If other lines of equipment are lost or abandoned, first-line gear gives the operator a chance to survive and escape would-be captors."

The boys, thrilled by the concept of captors, quieted to listen.

"Other items such as MREs, a pocket knife, and a dummy are also included. Second-line gear includes necessary extras carried in load-bearing equipment or tactical vests where they can be reached quickly. This includes five to seven magazines of ammunition, hand grenades, water, water purification tablets, and medical supplies."

The boys sat in wonder, their meals forgotten.

"Third-line gear is supplies needed for a specific mission, not critical for immediate use." He thought for only a moment before he had it. "Radios and batteries, Claymore mines, ponchos, water filters, and night-vision goggles. Medical Corpsmen also put their medical gear into this category." He watched his wife's face to see if he had forgotten anything.

Sharon could only keep a straight face for a moment before breaking into a beautiful smile. "Very good, Lieutenant Buckner. You may chow down now." Sharon handed him his plate.

"Dad, we didn't know you had to study too," Bobby said, solemnly gnawing a drumstick.

"I sure am," Riondro said. "It's important to know everything I can about the SEAL team before I take my big test."

"What else do you know?" asked Trent.

His father took a long drink of soda. "Well, I know that SEALS operate in small units, the smallest being the swim team, which consists of two operatives. If a team comes onto a beach from a combat rubber raiding craft, a swim team might go ashore beforehand to secure the beach and silence any guards in the vicinity."

A.K. Kuykendall

"Silence," Trent said, not understanding.

"Once the beach is secure, the rest of the team moves ashore. The total group size might be four or eight, depending on the mission."

"That's a lot of guys," Bobby said.

"Not compared to an entire beach of combatants," Riondro replied. "There are only eight SEAL teams in the Navy. Four are based in Coronado and four in Little Creek, Virginia. Each team contains six platoons attached to a naval special warfare squadron."

"Where'd you learn all this?" Trent asked.

Riondro caught his son playfully under the chin. "I learned it from my Dad."

"You had a Dad?"

"Trent," Sharon said.

"It's all right," Riondo said to his wife before turning his attention to his youngest son. "I sure did. He was a SEAL, too. He always told me that it took a special person to earn the honors. So, I learned everything I could so I could be just like him." He couldn't tell his sons everything. For one, that he had rebelled against his father, a Vietnam veteran. Everything that Commander Nathan P. Buckner tried to instill in his son had the odor of authority to the teenager. Despite his Silver Star and Medal of Valor, Commander Buckner was an interloper to his only child.

Before his teenage years, Riondro had idolized his father. The man would weave vivid tales of his tours in Vietnam. In the stories, the commander always came away without a scratch, though Riondro knew his father had a prosthetic leg. Riondro believed these wild tales and knew that someday, he would follow in his father's footsteps.

But during his late teenage years, Riondro had to witness his father—his teacher, his hero—lose his mind. For reasons the doctors weren't able to diagnose, the commander went from a powerful, intelligent father figure to a babbling madman, a danger to himself and others. He died alone in an institution. Riondro's mother, a political activist named Diana Christen Buckner, worked hard to act as both parents in the household, but her son was already lost, channeling his grief into binges of sex and drinking. He knocked up his seventeen-year-old girlfriend, who immediately threatened to disappear with the baby if he didn't fly right.

It was exactly the wakeup call he needed. He married Sharon three months before Bobby was born. The birth of his child marked his transition into adulthood and would define the rest of his life. He enlisted in the Navy the week after Bobby was born.

His mother moved on from her activist days to become an Alderman of District #87 of Amherst and eventually a candidate for governor. She had made plenty of enemies protesting the Vietnam War in her writing, including two books on Kennedy's assassination and a third on the hidden conspiracy behind the Vietnam War.

She was killed under questionable circumstances—hit by falling debris at a ribbon cutting ceremony—just two days before she was expected to be elected governor of New York State. She was ahead in the polls by sixty-eight percent and was assured to win by a landslide.

The boys were running around trees in the park, enjoying their boundless energy. Riondro realized they had been sitting in silence for some time and he looked at his wife, an apology in his eyes.

She reached over to grasp his hand. "What's that surprise you said you have for me tonight?"

"If I told you, it wouldn't be a surprise, would it?" He reached over to tickle her and they collapsed into one another, laughing like kids.

* * *

Pensacola Naval Base, Florida - August 1993

Coming out of a long, intense daydream, Lieutenant Riondro Buckner found himself sprawled on the ground. His nose was coated in blood and a fellow soldier stood over him, ready to deliver another blow. Buckner leapt to his feet and took the soldier to his knees with a throat-crushing maneuver as officers looked on, taking note of this lieutenant's fearlessness and drive.

5

General George Thimpkin was an anomaly since the day he was born. It was 1946, in Harmony Circle, a little town near San Diego, when Thimpkin's mother swears her baby was born saluting the doctor.

He grew up to pursue a career spanning over forty years, but started as an exceptional ROTC candidate who filtered into the Army at sixteen. He was declared a prodigy before he enlisted and had already worked with the Pentagon, troubleshooting and decoding international intelligence. He never failed.

His father, General Henry C. Thimpkin, was a highly revered four-star general, who had also come up in the decoding community. He was the only man to project the whereabouts of Japan's military fleet prior to Pearl Harbor, though his projections were overlooked by superior officers.

The elder Thimpkin was essential to the ongoing secret projects of Area 51. His primary duty was to recruit prodigy candidates worldwide in all areas of expertise to help study certain scientific anomalies on the base. The old general often told his brilliant son about another young man, a rocketry genius named David Adare.

Years before young Thimpkin was in diapers, his father sent seventeen-year-old David 82 floors down into the underground base.

There, the young man found, for his consideration, a biologically adaptable extraterrestrial entity in the form of a highly complex but utterly mystifying engine that could separate from the actual spaceship. David had about five minutes to evaluate the engine and took advantage of his time, crawling over it and making copious notes before he was told to step down. It would be his only trip to Area 51's testing sites.

What David didn't know was that he was a part of an experiment he hadn't anticipated; his superiors observed his interaction with the extraterrestrial technology, and had found that the device had the ability to change the psyche of anyone standing within eight feet. Every time a credible UFO sighting occurred anywhere around the world, the engine would react with what appeared to be emotion; colors flashed over its metallic surface. Base biochemists speculated the engine was a living organism controlled by the extraterrestrial pilots, seemingly symbiotic, and they wanted to test this theory with a human. General Henry C. Thimpkin himself observed David's interaction from a secure room nearby.

David reeled from the machine, pointing at the men in the room. "You people don't have the right to keep this technology from the American people," he yelled. "Humanity deserves to know!" The curious boy had transformed before their eyes. Further testing would eventually show that each time they brought an extraterrestrial close to the device, its activity increased to the point that no scientist could study the craft. The reaction was blinding. They speculated the earthquakes and massive storms plaguing the planet could be caused by the singular device, as if it had the power to absorb the whims of the earth itself.

But for the moment, a change would have to be made. Thimpkin glared at the raving young man. "He's out," the general growled. "Assign him with Rudolph." David Adare naturally understood the schematics of complex aerial craft and could sum up the highly technical operational fundamentals by memory alone. He was the kind of brilliant propulsion junky that would be a total asset to Special Cavalry Services Intelligence Department. Dr. Rudolph, Area 51's leading expert on propulsion-based aviation and biochemical weaponry, had absolute authority over the craft anomaly. He had always found David, the son of a colleague, to be an interesting young man and kept him under quiet observation since the boy was eight.

Years later, George Thimpkin was only a year old when his father took him to see the engine. The boy's eyes lit up and he reached out. "His mother's going to kill me," the general said as he held the child closer. Scientists who observed realized at once the anomaly was communicating with the boy. Data collected during that time was astonishing, and a communicative gate opened between the alien anomaly and the child. And just like that, young George Thimpkin became the youngest asset in American intergalactic intelligence.

* * *

By 1961, George Thimpkin was working on the Bay of Pigs project. Kennedy himself had gotten wind of Thimpkin's ability and knew that the teenager wasn't privy to every detail.

Increased friction between the United States and Castro's leftist regime had led President Dwight D. Eisenhower to break off diplomatic relations with Cuba in January of 1961. Even before that, the CIA was training anti-revolutionary Cuban exiles for a possible invasion of the island. Kennedy had approved the invasion, which had been designed as a means to overthrow Castro's regime without revealing the United States' involvement. The plan originally called for the gradual buildup of anti-Castro forces within Cuba, creating a cohesive political and military unit capable of toppling the leader. However, the operation quickly escalated into plans for a full-scale invasion, as the budget expanded from four million to forty-six million dollars, including funds for CIA training and support for anti-Castro Cuban exiles in Guatemala. On April 15, CIA pilots destroyed part of Castro's air force. They were preparing to complete the job on April 16 when President Kennedy ordered a halt to the air strikes.

On April 17, about fifteen hundred exiles, armed with American weapons, landed at the Bahía de Cochinos on the south coast of Cuba. Hoping to find support from the local population, they intended to cross the island to Habana. They failed, stopped by Castro's army. By the time the fighting ended on April 19, about one hundred men had been killed and the rest taken prisoner.

The invasion's failure seriously embarrassed the Kennedy administration, which was blamed by some for not providing adequate air support and by others for allowing it to take place at all. An internal CIA audit of the operation blamed the failure on a series of mistakes by the agency in planning and executing the invasion.

Prepared by CIA Inspector General Lyman Kirkpatrick, the audit was kept secret for thirty-six years before being released to the public in 1998.

Kirkpatrick concluded that the CIA failed to provide adequate security measures during mission training and prep. News of the impending invasion leaked to the media and subsequently reached Castro, who prepared for the attack. The audit also found that the CIA conducted little reliable intelligence gathering regarding the situation in Cuba and failed to realize that no wide-scale organized resistance to the Castro regime existed to assist the invaders. Despite this lack of intelligence, the agency assured Kennedy that an invasion would be met with strong support from the Cuban people; support which never materialized.

After the audit, one of the few loose ends in the invasion was why Kennedy chose not to strike on April 16. At the center of the secret was fifteen-year-old George Thimpkin. His infiltration of the CIA offered the proof Kennedy needed that a conspiracy was underway. Thimpkin discovered the conspirators planned to place another dictator in Castro's place so America would indirectly rule Cuba. This infiltration followed a pipeline all the way to important officials within Kennedy's cabinet. This information was never brought to the attention of the media or American citizens. Professionally, Kennedy felt it was his duty to maintain the sanctity of democracy by withholding this information; personally, he knew to keep his enemies close. Unfortunately, the conspirators' agenda would expand to include his assassination.

* * *

Cubans never stopped fighting for the liberation of their country, and the CIA performed more than 350 black ops missions to Cuba. As tensions mounted, the Cuban Missile Crisis became inevitable.

Although most people weren't aware, the crisis that shocked America was a long time coming. Castro had been a stateside pain in the ass when he confiscated property belonging to wealthy Cubans and foreigners in an attempt to improve conditions for poor and working-class Cubans. Many of the seized properties belonged to businesses owned by wealthy United States companies with strong political ties; ties which stretched all the way to the Oval Office.

The power struggle came to define the conspirators' coup against Kennedy. One short day before that ominous standoff between the United States and the USSR, Thimpkin attempted to send Kennedy a report that Castro had agreed, in confidence, to cease development of the weapons program with the USSR and their affiliation with Russia. It would have been a true peacekeeping coup, but certain men withheld this vital information from Kennedy.

The conspirators were itching to teach Castro a lesson, but they had no authority to wage war in Cuba without permission from the commander in chief. Their objective was to take down Castro and embarrass Kennedy, to teach him a lesson, and pitting the two men against one another was the perfect plan. Without Thimpkin's intelligence, it just might have worked.

That intelligence turned a frustrating chess game into a clear victory for the president. Kennedy would refer to his action in the Cuban Missile Crisis as a credibility reconstruction and a final conclusion to the Bay of Pigs.

After he successfully navigated the standoff, Kennedy would forever be remembered as a president who personified intelligence, honor, morals, and the strength of a nation—a president who had prevented the clear and present danger of nuclear war.

Thimpkin, on the other hand, was a mole. Kennedy knew he lived in a time of internal treachery and deceit. Because of this, he never disclosed Thimpkin's actions to anyone.

* * *

Lee Harvey Oswald was born on October 18, 1939, in a lower-middle-class family in a downtrodden New Orleans neighborhood. In January 1948, after the death of her fourth husband, Robert Edward Lee Oswald, Lee's mother Marguerite agreed to have her second son tested.

Although there was nothing wrong with Lee except his quiet nature, psychologists were promoting a program that would help "emotionally detached" children. They said the test subjects would have a chance to increase their body mass, intellect, and energy.

Nine-year-old Lee was a little small and skinny for his age, but Marguerite focused more on what was being offered. The facility paid in excess of one hundred dollars for every ounce of blood drawn from her son during the testing phase, not to mention forty-seven dollars for every hour he spent in testing. Marguerite's only duty was to keep her mouth shut about the experiment.

He entered a testing facility where children like him were exposed to a "new miracle drug." This experiment actually tested the first batches of a serum created in November 1947. Known as the Aneman Serum, it evolved from a top-secret National Security project, code-name The Aneman Project.

Since 1947, certain factions within the US government had conspired to create a serum with the sole purpose of injecting it into combat-trained military personnel. The serum would create a practically invincible soldier. Oswald was the only child out of the thirty-two test subjects who moved on to the second phase. His intellect increased tremendously and he was able to pick up languages flawlessly after only one day of observation. His hearing, sight, and speed increased as his tolerance for pain elevated. He could run for three miles without breaking a sweat.

One side effect monitored by the scientists was the tendency for patients to become explosive and aggressive. Oswald's drive for perfection increased; though he was the youngest member of the test group, he hated being referred to as an underdog.

His stint with the project ended on his tenth birthday. His mother earned $50,000 cash for her sacrifice. By the time he was seventeen, Oswald entered the Marine Corps, was court-martialed twice for confidential reasons, and experienced well-documented violent episodes and mood swings. His success in Aneman put him at the top of the government's protection list.

Oswald was indeed a dangerous man. With his advanced education and training made possible by the Special Cavalry Services Intelligence Agency, he was molded into a black ops soldier with a success rate of one hundred percent. He was a rare breed, but his military stint was only a front for his true objective.

He was a quadruple agent, playing the middle of every country in the world in the interests of the United States; the first of this experimental breed of superhuman soldier, but not the last. He could have ended Kennedy's life on his own, for he was an excellent shot—an enhanced marksman—yet that wasn't his objective. His true mission was to perpetrate a farce so his black ops comrades could do the deed and escape undetected, leaving Americans with an enigma never to be solved.

Oswald took his place on the sixth floor of the Texas School Book Depository. With gloves on so as not to leave any fingerprints, he set off three shots, purposely missing Kennedy and causing people to look in his direction. His Italian World War II Mannlicher-Carcano was loud and left a smoky trail. He left the nest, sped down the winding staircase, and planted himself in the lunchroom, where witnesses Marrion Baker and Roy Truly witnessed a calm gentleman—a man who was supposedly unaware the president had been shot just a few moments earlier, although the resulting pandemonium could be heard for more than half a mile.

The only information the government made public was Oswald's Russian involvement, inspiring the publication of more than two thousand books on Kennedy's assassination. Most of the documentation and speculations were backed by the same covert conspirators who orchestrated the operation.

Black ops agents live off the grid. They have no family, friends or conventional lives. They are ghosts—modern-day androids who follow any order given by their unknown superiors. One thing is always a given: an assassin never works alone.

* * *

The day President Kennedy was assassinated was one George Thimpkin would never forget.

Two days before, direct orders from Kennedy sent Thimpkin to Vietnam on a fact-finding mission. His orders were to monitor and categorize ongoing military actions. At 8:00 a.m. on November 22, 1963, Thimpkin reported his findings to Kennedy. As Thimpkin made his way out of Vietnam, he noticed tensions had increased among negotiators from both the Vietcong and the Americans.

Thimpkin noted in his report that the 16,200 troops stationed in Vietnam on support and assistance duties had recently been placed in ambush formation around essential operational points. To Thimpkin, it was clear that ground commanders, acting on unknown orders, were preparing for an all-out strike. With this new intelligence, Kennedy planned to remove the 16,200 troops from Vietnam effective November 25, 1963. Thimpkin was horrified by the assassination and even more shocked when he learned the supposed assassin was Lee Harvey Oswald. The face he saw plastered on television screens was the face of a man with forty-three names. Oswald was highly trained in black ops, a specialist trained in international infiltration.

Just like Thimpkin himself.

* * *

The black operations department of Fleet Cavalry's Special Services was seen as a necessary evil within the Armed Forces. Periodically, the federation council checked in to see that guidelines were being followed, and this afforded the Cavalry Black Operations a small window of opportunity to take care of the messier side of federation business. Although many black operation missions launched from General Frank's station, there was no official headquarters. Black ops met and operated anywhere they needed, depending on their mission.

Fleet Cavalry ships and units periodically took on black ops missions. Most assignments were on rotation, lasting up to six months per tour. Often, in these cases, only specifically placed officers knew their ship was assigned to black ops.

In addition to these random assignments, a small fleet of ships was permanently assigned to the department. The black ops fleet wasn't organized in standard military fashion, didn't contain specific ship classes and types, and the specific number of men and women assigned was unknown.

Black operations was backed by the intelligence department of Fleet Cavalry's Special Cavalry Services. Located on General Frank's station, the intelligence department focused on data-gathering operations in the frontiers of federation space and beyond. Officers and enlisted personnel of the intelligence department worked in the main office, on fleet cavalry and star fleet ships, and as operatives in all regions of the galaxy. The department of intelligence reported directly to the commander of the fleet cavalry and the cavalry operations director. All missions were sanctioned by these officers.

In most cases, intelligence personnel worked alone or in small teams known as cadres. Few intelligence missions covered more than data gathering. When situations required an extreme response, the black operations department was contacted and set into motion.

Most intelligence missions ran for six months to two years, depending on how deep an agent needed to go for data gathering activities. The intelligence department employed facilities for plastic surgery and other physical alterations. Still more facilities featured advanced training compounds.

Following Kennedy's assassination, the only time Thimpkin spoke to a civilian about the details of this event was to a man Thimpkin admired, New Orleans District Attorney Jim Garrison. Even with death breathing down his neck and the safety of his family an ongoing concern, Mr. Garrison tried to reveal a world of corruption and secrecy—a world of political upheaval, of murderous, contemptible, power-hungry political businessmen who craved superiority and pissed on the Constitution every morning of their egregious lives. Their corrupt actions led all the way up to Lyndon B. Johnson.

Oswald was not killed by Jack Ruby. In fact, he was assassinated years later in the Dominican Republic, on August 19, 1974, by members of a secret society called Fierce Chicanery. His assassination was cloaked as a lovers' quarrel. He was allowed to live as long as he did only because his contacts were of minor importance to the secret society. Oswald's contacts included the marksmen who shot John Kennedy. These men were a nuisance to this secret society and they also received a death befitting traitorous soldiers.

Fierce Chicanery's objective to date, besides complex highly sensitive national and international operations, was the strategic elimination or debunking of those individuals that took part in the coup that plotted and carried out the successful assassination. Members of this protective society included corporate businessmen, Republicans, Democrats, White House staff members, CIA agents, FBI agents, Secret Service agents, and military officers. Fierce Chicanery was forged out of a true drive for world peace and its influence stretched farther than the average man could imagine.

Prior to Oswald's true death, his appearance was drastically altered so he could continue his stint as a black ops agent.

* * *

On November 11, 1987, Thimpkin returned to Area 51, summoned by the alien technology his father exposed him to as a child.

The high-ranking general ordered scientists to open the bay doors and place the engine inside the hull. The scientists complied, citing Thimpkin's high clearance. Thimpkin entered the ship and took a seat as the door behind him sealed itself. He intended to fly the thing.

Moments later, a deafening roar scorched the surrounding area and the craft shot upward, disappearing from radar screens in less than six seconds. Before he could spit, Thimpkin found himself over Gulf Breeze, Florida. The flight was witnessed and caused a major controversy.

Thimpkin didn't realize he was in communication with other ships like the one he was in until they rallied around him over Gulf Breeze. "Return the ship to Area 51," the voices said, drawn directly into Thimpkin's mind. "The ship is biologically part of our brethren."

Thimpkin opened up a line of response. "But you called on me. I was drawn back to this ship and allowed to board and fly it. Why did you call on me?"

"Our brethren housed at your base are flying the ship you're currently occupying, at a great cost to their health, given the weakened state you humanoids have caused upon them. We did not call on you—our brethren did."

"But why?"

"Your journey here has given us all we need." The communication ceased. It was lonely there, in the silence.

When Thimpkin returned the ship and exited, the vessel sealed itself and from that moment no one was allowed to come within thirty feet of it—not even Thimpkin.

In the immediate debriefing, he chose not to disclose his communication with other ships and the beings they contained. He didn't ask about further clearance in Area 51 so he could see how they'd hidden the aliens they'd been keeping for God knew how long. Calm and collected, Thimpkin simply continued his regular duties. He knew how to play the game.

And so, though many of his missions were cloaked in secrecy, General George Thimpkin rose steadily through the ranks, finally gaining the status of post commander of the United States' infamous special ops training base, Post Base 22-987 Dingo. This base was the training grounds, communication center, and deployment center for special ops and intelligence. As he finally gained clearance to explore all areas of the connective Area 51, Thimpkin learned what had been hidden for more than eighty years.

* * *

Post Base 22-987 Dingo - October 3, 1998

Rhythmic steps echoed as Captain Flaker and General Thimpkin walked across the campus of 22-987 Dingo, surrounded by training troops and the day-to-day activities of the base's military personnel.

"I get the feeling this is anything but a leisurely stroll," Flaker said. "What is it you need from me?"

"I have an important mission for you, Captain. Our country needs you to fulfill a mission." Thimpkin showed her the folder in his hand. "It's of the utmost importance."

The two reached a bench in full view of a training team. Thimpkin gestured for her to sit. "We've known for years that we still have American prisoners of war in Vietnam," he said. "But this mission isn't rescue and recover; it's a murder exit. Your mission is to eliminate those soldiers."

Flaker raised an eyebrow. "You want me to murder our fallen soldiers?"

"That's correct. You and your team will rendezvous with the SEALs at Norfolk's Icehouse, where you'll be briefed on the mission by a friend and colleague of mine, Admiral Thunder Hamilton."

He leaned closer and lowered his voice. "Off the record, Captain, you and the team aren't expected to return after this. Once you confirm the fallen soldiers have been eliminated, an alert from our government will inform the Vietnamese consul that they have hostile forces in their territory. You and your troops will be in for the fight of your lives. Our government doesn't want you to come back. In fact, your chances of surviving are one in a million."

"Why are you telling me this?"

"Because I've known you since you were a pissed-off teenager, and I watched you grow into a beautiful woman and the best damn soldier I've ever known." He paused to light one of his Cuban cigars and took a few puffs, watching the training exercise as he spoke. "I chose you for this mission because you're the most likely person to make it out alive."

"With all due respect, sir, what about my team?"

He sighed. "I know the motherfucking Ranger's creed—hell, I practically wrote the book. I don't want you to come back to this outfit. Because of your mission, the government can't risk a leak in national security, not now, not ever. You are to complete the mission, and if you make it out, you'll disappear."

"What about the American POWs? Why kill them?"

"It's a matter of national security. Complete your mission, recover no one, and get the hell out of there."

Placing his cigar in his mouth, Thimpkin handed Flaker the folder. She scanned its contents as the general walked away in a cloud of cigar smoke.

* * *

Norfolk, Virginia - October 11, 1998

The next eight days passed all too quickly for Captain Flaker and her team. On Thursday evening, they bunked at the Icehouse for the last night before the mission began. An hour after nightfall, they met in a mission control bunker deep underground. The room was dark, lit only by a green glow from a screen at the front of the room.

Admiral Thunder Hamilton briefed Flaker and Lieutenant Riondro Buckner, who sat opposite him at the round table. The rest of the team stood in formation behind them. Staring at the admiral, Kalista realized his hooded eyes had seen things she could only imagine.

"Drop zone will be in the sixth quadrant at Anabald's Pier, seven miles from the war holes," Admiral Hamilton said. "A number of tactical tunnels survived the Vietnam War, and you will use them to your advantage."

The admiral sipped his coffee. "Your objective is a matter of national security. Therefore, I wasn't fully briefed. My duty is to provide your team with safe passage in and out of the Vietnamese territory." He moved to the diagram. "After you parachute in, you'll have a thirty-mile hike south, into enemy territory. Once there, you'll locate a spot at the base of a tree approximately forty kilometers to the east of the specified route. It will be marked with a yellow signal marker." He used a laser pointer to show the drop site on the map. "Dig here to find the opening to the tunnels. Once you breach the tunnel system, you'll find eighteen different tunnels going in many directions. You and your crew will fan out and look for the military drop box, which will contain your remaining instructions."

He took a seat and for a moment, returned a steady stare at Flaker. "I'll be your contact here at checkpoint and you need to keep an open line at all times," he said. "If you run into any problems, radio me at once and I'll give the order to abort. Good luck, team."

6

A black military cargo plane soared through the night, crossing the full moon and moving steadily eastward.

Inside its massive hull, Captain Flaker and Lieutenant Buckner introduced their team members. With less than twenty-four hours until they flew over the drop zone, team members sized each other up. The men and women aboard the transport were all between the ages of 24 and 36, strong and rough, each the best of the best.

Buckner addressed them. "Listen up! Obviously, merging two Special Forces teams from two different branches of our great military will create some friction along with it. But we have a mission to complete, folks, and that should be the only thing on our minds." He looked down at his roster and read aloud the names of his team.

Lieutenant Junior Grade Bobby Hascle: SEAL 53
Ensign Gregory Gull: SEAL 41
Ensign Victor Killoy: SEAL 40
Ensign Harry Smith: SEAL 31
Ensign Thankgod Emo: SEAL 32

Ensign James Betterman: SEAL 22
Ensign Aaron Yoo: SEAL 18
Ensign Daniel Haze: SEAL 16
Ensign Andrew Pierce: SEAL 12
Ensign Dick Wolf: SEAL 8

"Those numbers are not codes, people—they're body counts. The person you're looking at now may be the one who saves your life. If you have any beef with one another, I insist you squash them before we land."

The plane hit a sudden burst of turbulence. The soldiers grabbed ceiling harnesses to keep from falling.

Once the plane was steady again, Flaker addressed the unit. "This is a tough mission," she said, "but our objective is simple: find POWs held in Vietnam and eliminate them."

Flaker paused to allow her statement to sink in as the soldiers exchanged looks. She read from her own roll call:

First Lieutenant Frank Cassio—Ghost
Second Lieutenant Dave Scugs—Deno
Sergeant Major Vernin Tailhawk—Tracker
Sergeant Major Rick Drifuss—Force
Sergeant First Class Harry Loomis—X
Sergeant First Class Bobby Danials—Bobby Bullets
Sergeant First Class George Snuke—Crush
Sergeant First Class Sharon Whitmon—Lee
Staff Sergeant Dewane Mosely—Toom
Staff Sergeant Glory Numan—Man Z

Flaker stood at attention. "Rangers," she shouted. "Sound off!"

"Hooah! Hooah! Hooah!" the men returned.

* * *

Buckner knelt beside the door, shouting "Go!" to each man in line as they leapt from the plane. Flaker was the last one out.

He yelled louder to be sure he was heard above the noise of the engine and the rushing wind. "Captain, see you on the ground!"

She paused and met his eyes.

"What is it?" Buckner asked.

A moment of doubt crossed her eyes. It passed, and she clasped him on the shoulder. "Good luck!" she called out.

When she cleared the plane, Buckner signaled the all-clear to the pilots. "Mission clear. I'm out."

The captain answered with a high thumbs up, and Buckner jumped. The plane began a slow turn home.

7

General Thimpkin enjoyed two Cuban cigars a day. These imported treasures had been an addiction of his since his first mission to Cuba during the Missile Crisis. In fact, President Kennedy gave him his first box on a Tuesday evening in June 1962.

Kennedy also loved to smoke the Cuban critters from time to time—until one evening, when Bobby scared him off them by reminding him how their mother would stitch him good if she knew he was smoking. That very evening, Kennedy slipped his stash to Thimpkin, who was there to meet with a small unit of trustees. When the meeting ended, Bobby quietly asked Thimpkin if he could steal a couple of the stogies for himself.

The telephone interrupted General Thimpkin's daydreaming. He pushed a button and turned on the speaker. "Admiral Thunder!" he said. "It's been a long time. Was the drop successful?" Thimpkin asked. He took a puff of his cigar and held the smoke in. It was important not to seem too anxious.

"It was. The teams moved out at zero six hundred daybreak."

"Thunder, I'd like you to personally keep me informed of this mission's progress. Will you do that for me?"

"Sure, Butterfoot, but why is this mission so important to you? You're not getting soft on your troops, are you?"

"I run a tight ship because our country expects it," Thimpkin said, tapping his cigar into the ashtray. "That doesn't mean I don't care about my troops."

He stood, took what was left of his cigar, and ground it out. Strolling to the humidor, he selected another cigar, then gazed out the window. He gazed out his office window and wiped a bit of moisture from his face. His mind was already wandering to the first day he met an unmanageable seventeen-year-old named Kalista Flaker who defied authority with every breath she took. He remembered her fragility. She would frown at the slightest gesture of kindness. When he looked deep into her eyes, he saw a little girl crying.

She didn't like being touched in any way, not even a simple handshake. Like a young lioness, she protected her five-year-old little brother Reggie from everything—especially love. She believed all love would eventually prove false.

Reggie, on the other hand, seemed to reach out for love with every developing muscle in his body. He was too young to understand the dangers of the world that his big sister knew all too well. Even at his young age, Reggie seemed a little bizarre—rambunctious and high-strung—but eerily intelligent. He could fix just about anything and was a wiz with computers. Although he was only five when Thimpkin met him, Reggie demonstrated uncanny intellectual abilities. He could decipher codes, riddles, puzzles, and advanced scientific theories. He was an unlikely prodigy, but a prodigy nonetheless.

The first time Thimpkin saw Kalista and her brother together, he knew she wasn't up to the task of raising the boy. He also knew she'd never stop trying.

Orders from his superiors had led Thimpkin to discover this troubled teenager and her brother. Thimpkin himself was a fatherless soldier with no reason to live beyond his changing mission. Like most special agents, he could drop everything and disappear on a whim. Somehow, when he met Kalista and Reggie, an emotional bug slipped into his heart, softening him. These children instantly appealed to his aging warrior's heart.

When he met the children, he was on a mission. His orders were to seek out and eliminate a past Aneman Project candidate—one of the thirty-two test subjects from January 1948. The subject was Christopher Z. Flaker—Kalista and Reggie's father. Flaker was number 32, and he was the last in line for a swift elimination.

It was well documented that, other than Oswald, the test subjects experienced lifelong sterility. But subject 32, the man Thimpkin had observed for an entire week before moving in to complete his mission, had two children.

He posed as an official from the local health board and obtained blood samples from the children. In the samples, he found traces of an unknown strand of DNA. Both children were phase-one carriers of the Aneman Project. This was indeed an anomaly; something Thimpkin knew scientists in the Aneman Project hadn't projected. Thimpkin continued his ruse as a board of health agent; it was easy enough, as the parents were relatively absent. When he visited the home that day, he asked, Reggie if he knew anything about exotic foods—the kind of thing you wouldn't find at the school cafeteria.

"Yes." Reggie said, examining the kit Thimpkin had brought.

"I've always been fond of Russian foods. Tell me—what is kulich?"

Reggie frowned. "A tall cylindrical Russian cake. It's in the shape of a priest's hat, flavored with fruit, almonds, and saffron. It's the Russian Orthodox ceremonial dessert for Easter, decorated with the letters XB, signifying 'Christ Is Risen,' and traditionally served with paskha."

The embedded agent was amazed. *This young man belongs in someone's think tank*, he told himself.

Reggie laughed, breaking Thimpkin from his reverie. Suddenly their old black-and-white television came on and began flashing from channel to channel. Reggie had taken Thimpkin's classified experimental government-issue whisper phone—a prototype of the modern cell phone—and had somehow programmed it to act as a television remote. This was technology currently being tested in the field. The chances of this young man dissecting its properties in such a short time were unbelievable. Again, Thimpkin was stumped.

Kalista came home from school, throwing her backpack against the couch and startling Thimpkin. Snatching her brother away, she glared at the intruder. "What's your fucking problem?"

"No problem, young lady," Thimpkin responded, all the while gathering his things. "I was just heading out. Before I go, is there something you want to tell me?"

She was so small, standing there before him. "Listen, I'm almost out of here," she said. "Fuck this house, fuck my family. The only reason I'm still here is because I can't leave my brother."

"What are you afraid of?" Thimpkin asked softly.

Before she got to answer, Mr. and Mrs. Flaker came into the room and Kalista rose, taking Reggie with her to their bedroom without another word.

Thimpkin watched the sun set over a nearby junkyard. He'd bugged the home during his visit and could listen in on the family and figure out when the children would most likely be asleep.

Moments later, he heard a commotion from the house—the muffled sound of Kalista crying and screaming, the mother and father laughing.

Alarmed, Thimpkin approached the back door, silently entered, and moved through the house. Peering into Kalista's room, he was shocked to see her unconscious and bleeding on the rumpled bed, her inner thighs and body covered with whip marks and bruises. Reggie emerged from the closet, crying softly, and crawled over to his sister. He lay beside her on the bed, pulling the sheets over her naked body.

In all his assignments, this was the strongest emotion Thimpkin had ever felt. These children were living in hell.

Thimpkin made a momentous decision: he would eliminate his primary target and also Mrs. Flaker, because he could see she was party to the abuse. He used a common black op technique to kill the couple, staging their deaths as a murder-suicide.

He enacted his plan simply, while the children were at school. By the time they returned home, police had sealed the area and wouldn't allow them in to find their parents, the gun featuring both parents' fingerprints, their blood. After that, the children were placed in foster care until Kalista's eighteenth birthday, and then Reggie was legally under the care of his older sister. All the while, Thimpkin remained a steady professional presence, checking in on the kids after long missions abroad. Over time, he chipped away at the brick wall surrounding Kalista's feelings. Eventually she trusted him, and he became a close friend.

As Kalista entered the service and moved up the ranks, Thimpkin watched over her. She chose the life despite his attempts to dissuade her, and received no special treatment along the way; Thimpkin often told strangers that he hadn't met the woman until she arrived for the Best Ranger Competition. She was set on breaking away from the world she'd known and providing a secure home for herself and her brother. To fill time and further improve herself, she took college classes, studying the political, medical, and historical sciences. And, unsurprisingly, she turned out to be one hell of a soldier. She was focused—driven to succeed. Her need for perfection powered her drive, and anyone who served with her or under her command knew she was one badass, dick-in-the-dirt officer who would never ask a soldier to do anything she wasn't willing to do herself.

8

The troops prepared to move out at daybreak, strapping on their gear from a small base camp. Both teams readied their weapons and satellite communications in preparation for the mission ahead.

Captain Flaker did a final check of her own gear. "Tracker? SEAL 32?" she asked, a sense of urgency betraying the quiet morning.

"Yes, Captain?"

"I want you two scouting two miles south, then hold your positions, and if at all possible radio the all-clear. If you run into problems, fall back in double-time. Understood?"

"Yes, Captain." SEAL 32 and Tracker shuffled their gear and moved out.

"Hey, what is it with those pretty boy Rangers and their names?" SEAL 22 asked with a smirk. The other SEALS laughed. "Ghost? Tracker? Sounds like something out of a cartoon."

Without hesitation, Ghost dropped his gear and got into SEAL 22's face. The other SEALS gathered behind SEAL 22. The other Rangers looked on but held their positions.

"Want to know why they call me that?" Ghost threw a quick grin to his squad then swung back around to glare at SEAL 22. "That's ironic, because your mother wanted to know that very same thing before you were conceived!"

The Rangers and a couple SEALS laughed under their breath.

SEAL 22 came back a little sharper. "Whatever, Casper the friendly bitch," he said. "Why do they call you Ghost?"

Noticing that Ghost had dropped something at his feet, SEAL 22 leaned down to retrieve it—the other SEALS eyes followed. When he stood again, Ghost was gone. There was a noise behind them and when the men turned, they saw Ghost standing at their rear with a rocket launcher cocked, loaded, and ready to fire.

"I hope you water guppies aren't this slow out in the field," Ghost said with a smirk on his face as he widened the scope with one hand while massaging the trigger with the other. The entire Ranger team doubled over laughing.

Lieutenant Buckner walked into camp, Flaker right behind. "What's going on?" Buckner asked.

"We were just fucking around," SEAL 22 said.

"I don't believe fucking around is part of this mission," Buckner said.

Flaker frowned at Ghost. "Put down that goddamn rocket launcher before we go knuckle to knuckle."

"Immediately, Captain!"

* * *

Tracker and SEAL 32 scurried over the ground sixty feet short of their two-mile objective ahead of base camp.

SEAL 32 stopped Tracker for a quick breather. "It's hotter than hell out here," SEAL 32 said, pulling out his canteen to take a swig before dousing himself. "I could cook pasta with this water." Tracker nudged SEAL 32 and pointed.

"Lay off," the SEAL said. "You're spilling my shit."

"You'll spill your shit all over the fucking jungle if you're not careful," Tracker said, his voice a whisper. "Look up there."

SEAL 32 followed Tracker's gaze to find a well-hidden booby trap high in the trees. A thin black wire ran up into the branches, connecting to a spiked log about twelve feet in diameter and five feet in width. The trap was old and the spikes seemed a little wilted, but the device could definitely still fuck someone up. At ground level, the line was harnessed between two trees, with a tripwire that rested gently atop two weather-beaten land mines. Altogether, it was an old but highly effective booby trap with some hidden surprises.

"Goddamn," SEAL 32 said, taking it all in. "These fuckers act like they're still at war."

"It does seem like someone's expecting trouble." Tracker said, picking carefully at the booby trap.

"If I had to guess, I'd guess they were protecting something."

"Is it just me, or does your gut tell you this mission seems like something out of a Stephen King novel?"

"I don't read Stephen King's shit—overcompensating nerd. I'm a Koontz fan."

"Koontz? Now I know you're fucking crazy."

Hearing a rustle in the bushes off to the right, the men dropped flat on the ground. Seconds later a weasel scurried past, a mouse in its jaws.

"We're getting jumpy," Tracker muttered, standing and brushing himself off.

"Are you fucking kidding? I'm about to pass out."

The men finished disarming the bomb with a professionally placed clip from wire cutters. Tracker tied down the wire.

"I could water this entire jungle with the sweat dripping from my balls," said the SEAL.

"You should be a comedian."

"Funny you say that—I do standup during my R&R. Vegas. The Improv. Women love it."

"No shit?" Tracker said with a smile. "I might just check out a show one day."

"Don't expect any discounts—I don't know you," SEAL 32 said, grinning.

* * *

Bird sounds and other wildlife made the surrounding jungle feel like a living creature. As the two men disarmed their 46th booby trap, they realized they'd reached their ordered checkpoint.

Tracker radioed back to base, brushing a swarm of tiny bugs away from his face.

"Tracker, is that you?" a voice returned from camp.

"Lee! What's up, girl? We've scouted two miles ahead."

Lee ducked her head into the leaders' tent. The two looked up from a route map. "Excuse me, Captain—Lieutenant? Tracker and SEAL 32 are at point and they're on the line."

"Patch it through," Flaker said.

Buckner placed the radio on the speaker.

"Gentlemen!" he said. "Is the path secure?"

"Yes, but the plains have a lot of old booby traps and mines," SEAL 32 returned. "They're old but still battle ready with just enough sting to do the job. We disassembled forty-six and cleared a path. We strongly suggest clearing the entire perimeter. It's too hairy out here."

"You did stay along the southern plains as ordered?" Flaker asked.

"Yes, Captain," Tracker quickly answered, already feeling SEAL 32 was hogging all of what little glory they had earned.

"That was a commendable suggestion, SEAL 32," Flaker responded. The SEAL beamed.

"Okay," Flaker said. "I want you two to move out, secure the rest of the way, and report. Understood?"

"Yes, Captain."

"Any trouble, fall back. Be careful. Base out."

The line disconnected.

"You don't have to hog all the cake, man," Tracker said, loading his pack up. "What can I say? I was hungry."

"Seriously, asshole."

"Cut me a break. There's no glory in taking point in an informative correspondence to our superiors. I hope I'm not sensing a case of low self-esteem on your part."

"You better be glad I've come to like you, man."

* * *

Back at base camp, Buckner mustered the geared-up teams. "We're moving out! SEAL 12 and Force, secure the camp. Teams, assemble formation for Captain Flaker's orders."

"All ensigns will hold flank. Specialist, you lead. The rest will hold a circular formation," Flaker said. "Teams, move out!"

Within minutes the camp was vacated and any hint of their presence had been erased. The soldiers were about to undertake a mission they considered unbelievable: eliminate captive Vietnam veterans for unknown reasons.

The elite soldiers steadily pushed on.

9

Inside the Gecko Bravo Branch of the National Security Agency, a group of men and women were dealing with a crisis.

The group gathered at a round table. The tabletop was covered with a glossy, medieval design and the chairs were black leather. A pink marble floor, crystal chandelier, and sterling silver water pitchers gave the room an elegant feeling. The dark walls made it resemble Batman's cave.

The group listened on the speakerphone as Damion Walker conversed with General George Thimpkin. Walker was the head agent for the Gecko Bravo Branch, a focused, clean-cut gentleman with jelled black hair and dark features. He sat at the head of the round table, smoking a cigarette and fiddling with a sterling silver Zippo.

"General, I take it the teams are in the dark about the full mission."

"Yes, Mr. Walker." Thimpkin sat alone in his office at Post Base 22-987 Dingo. "The teams must be completely wiped out upon mission completion. There cannot be any returns. If that should happen, we'll eliminate them ourselves."

"Of course," the general answered. "If that's all, Mr. Walker, I have a schedule to keep and troops to evaluate."

Walker took a final drag of his cigarette and stubbed it out in a silver ashtray. "We understand, General. You must get back to your duties. We'll be in touch."

"I'm sure you will."

When Walker hung up, Debra Hilton—a tall, sleek blonde—said, "We might have to eliminate him as well."

Ingro nodded from the other side of the table. He was a rough-looking man with a solid silver eye patch glittering over his left eye. An old knife wound left a jagged scar beginning at his forehead and running straight down his face. He was Walker's leading assassin.

"I think you're right," Ingro said. "He seems a little too edgy about this whole project. Do you think he's mentioned anything?"

"He'll obviously have to be eliminated," Walker said, "along with anyone else associated with this mission outside our branch. Excluding, of course, our Washington liaisons."

"Everyone?" asked Ingro.

"Everyone associated with the project at any level will have to be eliminated." Walker lit another cigarette. "Once the teams complete their objectives, they've been instructed to contact Admiral Hamilton. Then, he and his port team will be eliminated, followed by Thimpkin. With one call to the Vietnamese consul, we all know the mission teams won't make it out alive."

* * *

Around the same time General George Thimpkin was privileged with the opportunity to head Post Base 22-987 Dingo, Damion Walker was taken off the black ops roster to join a venture that made him a front man for a highly confidential mission of the National Security Council.

Walker served as head of a unit that was actually a secret extension of the Special Cavalry Service, a new division known as the National Security's Gecko Bravo Branch. Walker's promotion to leading agent of this branch was for one purpose only: to continue an objective he'd taken part in during his tenure as a Special Cavalry Services black ops agent. Walker's primary duties dealt with the continued research and development of a serum by way of Project Aneman.

Although he was eight years younger than General Thimpkin, Damion Walker was a force to be reckoned with. Thimpkin knew him all too well. Walker had a streak of evil so menacing that when he stood next to a glass of water, this fuck could turn it into a cylinder of ice.

Throughout the many assignments he'd held in various covert institutions, Thimpkin made it his job to keep an eye on would-be threats. During his tenure as President Kennedy's mole, he had little insight into the Special Cavalry Services black operations—until Kennedy fell to the assassin's bullet.

When the assassin was proclaimed to be Lee Harvey Oswald, Thimpkin knew Walker, who was only nine years old at the time, was Oswald's handler. Oswald was a special case—an Aneman subject. It was a hard lesson, but it taught Thimpkin to keep his enemies close.

With a loveless upbringing, Walker had been groomed from birth by genetic scientists of the Special Cavalry Services in an unsanctioned program experimenting with mind control. Thimpkin was aware that grooming children from birth was a government undertaking, which spans generations. Walker excelled!

Walker, at age seven, had been assigned to a special black ops task force in November 1961 to head up a highly confidential covert tactics operation. This operation was far off the scope of black ops' usual agenda. Instead of operating in international and diplomatic affairs, Special Cavalry Services Black Operations was planning something backed by unknowns at clearance levels higher than the president himself.

Though Thimpkin had his hands in practically every covert operation in recent years, he'd known nothing of the mission that led to the execution and subsequent cover-up.

Without realizing what was happening, Thimpkin was slowly being converted from a covert think tank draftee to a permanent black ops field agent. Walker knew this and purposely kept Thimpkin in the dark.

In his personal investigation after the Kennedy assassination, Thimpkin found that Special Cavalry Services didn't even have the balls to classify the mission, creating a paper trail would surely have led all the way up the line.

Thimpkin despised their actions. However, as a career tactics specialist for the Special Cavalry Services, he found the conspirators' coup to be ingenious. It was the perfect murder and subsequent smokescreen that was sure to hold for generations on end as, unbeknownst to anyone, it was a child (Walker) who delivered that fatal shot to the cranium of President Kennedy from a vantage point he could only fit comfortably—the storm drain location.

Walker was the perfect candidate for that operation. He was also the perfect candidate to head up the Gecko Bravo Branch, for they needed a coldhearted, lifeless android like him. The only reason Walker wasn't snuffed out by agents of Fierce Chicanery long ago was the fact that in his current position, he unknowingly catered directly to their ongoing objectives.

Thimpkin and Walker's last mission together was on June 17, 1972. On that day, one incident forged a permanent wedge between the two men. Thimpkin already despised this bloodthirsty vampire, but on this mission, Walker proved to be a real back-stabbing little shit.

It was a politically driven mission from start to finish, and Thimpkin was ordered to head it. He was charged with planning and executing a burglary of the Democratic Party's National Committee offices at the Watergate Hotel in Washington, D.C. Although he had serious doubts about the mission and only received limited authority to pick his own team, Thimpkin agreed to go forward, fearing his reputation would be diminished if he refused.

When he learned the crazy fuck Walker would be his number one, Thimpkin was floored. Walker was on Fierce Chicanery's hit list! Thimpkin reasoned that the mission would make a perfect cover for Walker's execution.

In truth, this was the break Fierce Chicanery had been waiting for. It provided a perfect opportunity to corrupt government officials all the way up to the White House. These were the same officials who had plotted Kennedy's assassination, including one of Lyndon B. Johnson's cohorts, Richard Milhous Nixon. The Watergate mission was meant to taint Nixon's reputation.

However, the plan fell short. Walker made it out of the Watergate Hotel unscathed, leaving Thimpkin to eat a bullet. Walker had ordered Eugenio Martinez to put one between Thimpkin's eyes and leave him dead inside the Democratic Party National Committee's office. Martinez informed Thimpkin of this plan as he held a pistol to Thimpkin's forehead and told him to drop to his knees.

Martinez was one of the five convicted burglars in the Watergate scandal. He worked for Barker's Miami real estate firm, had CIA connections, and was an anti-Castro Cuban exile. Hearing a noise outside the door, Martinez was distracted for a split second. In that moment, Thimpkin grabbed the weapon from his hand and punched Martinez in the face.

When officers broke into the office, they found five assailants, including Bernard L. Barker, a realtor from Miami and a former CIA operative. Barker was said to have been involved in the Bay of Pigs incident in 1962. They also captured Virgilio R. Gonzales, a locksmith from Miami and a refugee from Cuba; and James W. McCord, a security coordinator for the Republican

National Committee and the Committee for the Reelection of the President. McCord was also a former FBI and CIA agent. He was dismissed from his RNC and CREEP positions the day after the break-in. The last man in the room was Frank A. Sturgis, another associate of Barker's from Miami, also with CIA connections and involvement in anti-Castro activities.

The five men were charged with attempted burglary and attempted interception of telephone and other communications. The burglars were indicted by a grand jury. Also indicted was G. Gordon Liddy from Washington, counsel to the Finance Committee to Reelect the President, a former FBI agent, Treasury official, and member of the White House staff. During the investigation, Liddy refused to answer questions and was fired. E. Howard Hunt Jr., a former White House consultant and CIA employee, was also indicted. Hunt wrote espionage novels and had worked on declassifying the Pentagon Papers.

Thimpkin, an infiltration expert, escaped from the Watergate complex without a problem. His plan was executed flawlessly, giving Fierce Chicanery yet another victory. Watergate entered the political lexicon as a term synonymous with corruption and scandal. Had it not been for the actions of Frank Wills, a security guard and the carefully placed hero in Thimpkin's orchestrated takedown, the scandal might never have emerged.

By early 1974, the nation was consumed by Watergate. This had always been the mission of Fierce Chicanery: to expose the corrupt doings of government officials to the American public.

At 9:00 p.m. on the evening of August 8, 1974, Nixon delivered a nationally televised resignation speech. The next morning, he made his final remarks to the White House staff before sending his resignation letter to the secretary of state. Fierce Chicanery carefully watched this ordeal unfold, as every day brought the exposure of more political corruption. Their secret society was hugely successful as the conspirators' coup kept growing larger.

Watergate had profound consequences in the United States, with a long list of convictions and other casualties. The aftermath of Watergate ushered in changes in campaign finance reform and a more aggressive attitude by the media.

The scandal exposed the dark underbelly of politics to the American public. Suddenly, the United States was known throughout the world for political burglary, bribery, extortion, telephone tapping, conspiracy, obstruction of justice, and destruction of evidence, not to mention tax fraud, illegal use of government agencies such as the CIA and the FBI, illegal campaign contributions, and the use of public money for private purposes. Most of all, it exposed the state's blatant abuse of power.

After the fact, Walker made a point of avoiding Thimpkin. Although Walker was scheduled for execution by Fierce Chicanery, this proved difficult to achieve because of his affiliation with the National Security Agency. Within three years of the Watergate scandal, Walker was drafted by the NSA to head up the newly formed Gecko Bravo Branch. This was around the same time General Thimpkin was asked to step away from his duties with the Special Cavalry Services in order to head up Post Base 22-987 Dingo as post commander.

Damion Walker's new role led Fierce Chicanery to abandon their plans for his execution. At the Gecko Bravo Branch, he continued planning and development of the Aneman Project. It was an objective Fierce Chicanery had followed closely since the project's inception.

10

Norfolk, Virginia - October 12, 1998

"Checkpoint to mission?" Admiral Hamilton sent a numbered code to a secured line.

Lieutenant Buckner immediately retrieved the line. "Securing the line—" he responded quickly and began punching the code on his module, confirming its authenticity.

Moving steadily through the sweltering, bug-infested jungle, Buckner gestured at Captain Flaker to bring the team to a halt. Flaker called the team to an abrupt stop by using a subtle birdcall, a high fist, and a parallel flat hand to bring the soldiers to one knee. She then indicated they should stand fast, keeping on tight lookout as they silently but swiftly hit the dirt, weapons ready, peering through their high-tech scopes.

Buckner received his code confirmation and the line was cleared. "Mission here. Lieutenant Riondro Buckner."

"This is Admiral Hamilton. Any problems, Lieutenant?"

"Negative, sir. At this time, we are three miles from point. Once we hit point, we will have to temporarily clear the lines."

"Why is that?"

"We picked up a lot of radio interference prior to securing the lines when we first dropped. We can't take the chance our frequency will be traced. I have one of my men running a complete diagnostic, and the problem should be handled soon."

"Requesting immediate radio communication prior to the breach of the war holes. It's imperative that I'm able to communicate with this mission. Is this understood?"

"Affirmative!"

"Checkpoint, out."

The admiral disengaged. While putting away the line, Lieutenant Buckner turned to SEAL 12. "Double-time it on that diagnostic, I need it by point."

"Yes, sir."

SEAL 12 handed Flaker a repaired and isolated line. "Captain, I have that line cleared you requested. It's frequency 60.85."

"Thank you, Ensign," Flaker said. She called Tracker and SEAL 32. "We're two and a half miles from point and closing," she said. "Did you locate the signal marker?"

"Affirmative, we have cleared the opening," Tracker returned.

Flaker flipped up her canteen, took a quick swig, and doused herself in the warm water. "Good work. We're closing in. Keep the lines clear and sit tight. Mission out."

Half an hour passed. Tracker and SEAL 32 were on a tight lookout for the rest of the team when a series of birdcalls echoed through the jungle. Tracker sent out a single birdcall, giving the team the all-clear as they moved through the brush.

The teams immediately started setting up surveillance. Flaker and Buckner climbed into the burrow, scouting for the military drop box. They located the box and after opening it, discovered the exact location of the camp as well as the rendezvous location of their helicopter pickup.

Immediately after reading the lift information, Buckner motioned for SEAL 12 to come into the burrow.

SEAL 12 handed his superior the communication connector. Buckner turned toward Flaker, who was standing in front of the tunnels inside the burrow. He saw she was distracted, staring at the tunnel's entrance, and assumed she was contemplating technical matters.

In truth, she was thinking about her place in the Corps universe. The Ranger's Creed looped inside her head.

The last line particularly interested her that afternoon: *Readily will I display the intestinal fortitude required to fight onto the Ranger objective and complete the mission, though I be the lone survivor.* Flaker contemplated the creed she vowed to uphold until her death. She thought about her conversation with General Thimpkin before he gave her command of this unbelievable operation. She couldn't shake the fact that if she followed Thimpkin's orders in this mission, their fate was sealed.

She found herself doing something she'd vowed never to do—questioning her duty.

Thimpkin always spoke against this questioning as if it was a mortal sin, and she agreed with him. After all, he was her mentor, confidante, and friend. But something was wrong. Her duty went up against the unbelievable intel Thimpkin gave her in their last encounter.

She thought back further, to the day she told him she wanted to become a soldier. "You made your choice and I'll back you one hundred and twenty percent," he had said. "But be forewarned—I expect great things of you, and the Corps will expect twice as much. Remember one thing in your journey into hell. Orders are not debatable. Becoming a soldier means your choices are no longer your own. Your emotions must be set aside, for you may be required to perform unthinkable acts. I will always be your friend. When placed in harm's way, you must rely on the only friend you ultimately have—yourself."

Thimpkin's warnings flowed through Flaker's mind as she stared at the tunnels before her. She broke from her reverie to see Buckner standing in front of her. "I'm sorry, what is it?" she asked.

Buckner held out the communicator. "We're expected to report. The lines are clear and we're ready to push on with this mission. It's now 0900. We're expected to rendezvous at the pickup site two miles west of the southern plains—Captain, is something wrong?"

Flaker was drifting again, visions of her father flooding her mind. Every muscle in her body tensed.

Buckner lightly touched her shoulder. "Captain?"

In a single smooth action, she flipped him onto his back, then drew her knife and placed it at the base of his throat, within inches of his protruding Adam's apple.

Buckner grabbed Flaker's knife-wielding hand and slowly forced it away from his throat as they glared at each other.

"Captain Flaker, stand down!" Buckner shouted. "I don't know what's wrong with you! We have a mission to complete."

Within seconds, her eyes focused on his face. He stood, brushing himself off. "If you don't feel you can complete this mission, relieve your command."

Flaker blinked, looking around, her breathing ragged. Her expression changed from anger to confusion and she slowly replaced her knife in its sheath. "I'm sorry, Lieutenant. I can't explain what just happened, but I promise it won't happen again."

Buckner sized her up. His life was essentially in her hands, and he couldn't determine her mental state. Unfortunately, there wasn't much they could do about it in the jungle. He certainly couldn't send her back to base. They had to press on. "I won't pull rank and relieve you of command," he said, "but keep yourself under control. Communications are back on line. Would you like to check into base, or would you like me to?"

"I'll contact the base, Lieutenant," Flaker said, bewildered, her head aching.

"Affirmative, Captain." Buckner handed her the communicator.

* * *

Admiral Hamilton was alerted to Captain Flaker's communication and took the call at once.

"Captain, I take it your teams have finally made point," Hamilton said, sipping his coffee. "I was a little worried; you're almost behind schedule. I take it you're ready to push on?"

"Affirmative. We're set to go."

"You have your green light. We're all set to monitor from here. Keep communications on at all times, soldier. Once you complete your mission, you're to double-time it back; it's two miles on the entrance trail to the open fields where you rendezvous with your chopper. Understood?"

"Understood."

"Base out," Hamilton said.

* * *

From Walker's office at the Gecko Bravo Branch, the disconnecting click of a speakerphone sounded. Walker deactivated the eavesdropping device and stood to face his company of agents.

"You heard it, Ingro. Lead the team. Eliminate Hamilton and Thimpkin immediately. No witnesses."

"Yes, Mr. Walker." Ingro pushed away from the table.

"The rest of you are dismissed," Walker said.

11

The Icehouse was located in a secure, isolated area. It was designed for the classified deployment of special ops on low-profile operations. With frequent operations in play, Special Cavalry Services often used the site to launch their classified operations. As with all deployment sites, this was a secure and well-guarded operational point.

It was a surprise to everyone on location when the outer gate burst open and soldiers in black combat gear rushed inside, guns drawn.

Hearing men shouting outside his office, Admiral Hamilton ran for his door. What he saw knocked the wind out of him; he watched as his base operation team was heartlessly, efficiently eliminated with little to no return fire. His office personnel had been armed, but they obviously weren't expecting such an intense firefight—any firefight at all—in the reception area.

Hamilton knew Operation Rendezvous was in play; the birds were in the air. He had been eagerly awaiting a confirmation from the rendezvous choppers that were supposed to be en route to a secure location where they would extract the mission teams from Vietnam. Thinking quick, he suspected his call had been intercepted and overridden.

He slammed the office door shut, locked it, and rushed to his desk, where he grabbed his semiautomatic chrome-plated pistol from the top drawer, then ducked under his desk with the telephone. His only call was to General Thimpkin's direct line.

"This is Thimpkin."

"Thunder here." Hamilton kept his voice low. "George, my command's under attack. My men are being slaughtered like cattle. What the fuck is going on?"

"Where did you designate the mission's rendezvous?"

"What?" Hamilton shouted against the noise.

"The teams! Where is the rendezvous?"

"The team is on the border of the southern Vietnamese plains. They're expected to rendezvous two miles—"

Hamilton's office door burst open. A soldier pulled him from under his desk. Hamilton raised his weapon and put a round into the man's skull. Blood, bone, and brain matter splattered over his desk as the man crumpled to the ground.

Seven more men entered his office, six aiming their firearms at him. Standing in the middle of these armed men was Agent Doug Ingro.

Hamilton opened his mouth in disbelief. In a sudden wave, he remembered a classified Vietnam operation in 1967, when he was a young lieutenant. Doug Ingro was an ensign in his regiment. He discovered Ingro had raped and killed Petty Officer First Class Daria Coleman during that mission. When Ingro was court-martialed, he received nothing more than a slap on the wrist and was honorably discharged. It came as a shock to Hamilton, who had heard that the discharge—and perhaps the crime itself—had come as an order from higher up.

"You low-level piece of shit," Hamilton said.

Ingro laughed. "Admiral, it's not like you didn't do your share of dirt to get here."

"You crazed, son of a bitch. You raped and killed an outstanding soldier. Fucking psychopaths like you belong in the Mafia."

"You're right about Daria—she was outstanding. I showed that bitch the true meaning of pleasure and pain."

Hamilton clenched his fists. "You son of a bitch!"

"Anyway, you were right—I didn't belong in the Corps. I belonged exactly where I was placed."

"And where's that, you fucking piss ant?"

"Sticks and stones, Admiral. I'm afraid that information is classified." He smirked at the soldiers flanking him. "Take him out."

Hamilton raised his gun but it was too late. As he dropped to the ground in a pool of blood and gore, Ingro maneuvered around his body and hung up the phone. Outside, Ingro radioed Gecko Bravo headquarters. "Mr. Walker, Thunder is down. We're en route to General Thimpkin's locale."

* * *

Gecko Bravo Headquarters - 0952

Back at the Gecko Bravo Branch, Damion Walker was meeting with a group of agents in his office.

"Hilton, scramble the sweeper team and move out now," Walker said.

"Yes, sir."

Walker stood with a sigh. Behind him sat Greg Numan, his key Washington liaison posing as one of his agents in order to keep an eye on Project Aneman.

"Mr. Numan," Walker said, lighting a cigarette.

"Sir?"

"The tap on the mission communications; is it monitoring properly?"

"Yes, sir. The teams are in the camp as we speak. There's nothing abnormal on the open line. I don't think any of the mission team has any idea what's going on."

Walker spun to face the man. "You're not here to think, you fucking son of a bitch. You're here to see that this mission remains foolproof."

Walker turned to the others in the room. "All of you get the fuck out of here! Mr. Numan—all of you."

Alone, Walker took another drag of his cigarette.

* * *

Post Base 22-987 Dingo - 0948

General Thimpkin dialed the base's air traffic control unit and paced the floor in his office, carrying a lit cigar in his hand.

"Air traffic control, Sergeant Burrows speaking."

"Sergeant, this is General Thimpkin."

"Yes, sir. What can I do for you, sir?"

"I have an immediate confidential assignment for you. Call it a favor for getting you the night shift."

"Yes, sir."

"I want you to scramble two Sikorsky Pave Hawk helicopters, pilot Sergeant Major Harold Holang, and shooter Second Lieutenant David Thousin, to be assigned to the lead chopper. I'll be the shooter in the second chopper. All you have to do is to find me an excellent pilot, preferably a new jack pilot looking to make a name for himself." He paused. "Delay that last order. Have you heard of Sergeant Major Dick Mirrors?"

"Who hasn't, General? He's in the brig for his role in Operation Black Bumble last month in Guatemala. It would take an act of Congress to spring him out of that cage, sir."

"Consider this order your act of Congress. I want you to rally him as my pilot for this operation immediately. You got that?"

"Affirmative, General."

"Also, get me a full line of battle gear. Details of this mission are not to be mentioned to anyone, not even your immediate superiors. This mission is classified Operation Gold Star, effective immediately. If anyone requires further confirmation of my orders, tell him or her to contact me, but let them know they should be ready to step down from whatever title they currently hold. Do I make myself clear, Sergeant?

"Crystal clear, General."

"Good, I'll be there in less than thirty minutes."

"Sir?"

"Is there a problem?"

"No, sir! It's just that it will take some time to—"

"Upon my arrival, have the choppers fueled and my battle gear prepped and ready for me for when I arrive at the hangar. I'll suit up upon my arrival. Hooah!"

"Hooah, General."

Thimpkin paged his secretary. "Private Andrews, have a driver meet me in front with a jeep in three minutes. I'm flying to Washington for a presidential conference."

* * *

The national security hit teams were already en route to General Thimpkin's base. Agent Doug Ingro addressed the pilot, screwing a silencer onto his handgun. "How long until we get there?"

"Approximately forty minutes, sir."

"Make it twenty."

"Sir?"

"Just do it, goddammit!"

* * *

Post Base 22-987 Dingo - 1000

General Thimpkin sat in the backseat of a Jeep headed toward the helicopter flight field, holding a locked metal case in his lap.

The young driver glanced at him in the rear view mirror. "So, General, this must be important, sir, you being in a hurry and all. May I inquire—"

"Private, just drive the damn Jeep."

"Sorry, sir."

When they arrived at the airfield, Thimpkin geared up. Sergeant Burrows met him in front of the hangar, smiling from ear to ear like the ass-kissing simpleton he was. Thimpkin handed Burrows a folder with CLASSIFIED stamped on the front.

"Here are the area charts. I take it you mobilized the Sikorsky Pave Hawk helicopters as I requested?"

Sergeant Burrows quickly examined the folder's contents. "Of course, sir, but it will take some time to get to the —southern plains of—Vietnam, sir?"

"I've got two teams stranded out there, and I'll be damned if they're going to meet their maker on my watch."

Thimpkin saw the Sikorsky Pave Hawks, in formation and ready for flight. He sighed. "You remember the final words of my pledge, Sergeant?"

"Yes, sir, I do."

"Quote those words."

Burrows cleared his throat. "The lives of my soldiers make a superhero of me, especially when those lives are on the brink."

Thimpkin checked the two choppers as Holang, Thousin, and Mirrors filed out of the hangar. He attached two flat oval metallic objects to the surface of both aircraft.

Mirrors watched him do it. "Sir?"

"Sergeant, what you're looking at is top secret. You need to have faith in your general to get the job done."

"Yes sir, General."

* * *

Vietnamese Prison Camp - 0940

The prison camp was badly weathered and worn-down, built decades ago with no signs of an update. Grass-lined bamboo huts served as both the command center and the barracks.

The center of camp seemed to be where the true atrocities were performed. In it, six American POWs—old men, identifiable only by their bloated, filthy uniforms—dangled from a tall wooden support with hooks jabbed into their backs. Each man suffered under about twenty hooks. Captain Flaker noted through her binoculars that the men's feet and arms were hacked off, and flies swarmed around their wounds.

Two of the men were still, slumped at the end of their lines. The rest moaned in pain, fighting weakly. Flaker lowered her binoculars in saddened disbelief. Those men should have bled to death years ago, with those limb wounds. She shuddered to think of the torture the men must have endured. As the rest of the team emerged from the tunnel and fanned out to line the camp with explosives, Flaker and Lieutenant Buckner made their way toward the huts.

Flaker signaled Buckner to check the eight to the left while she checked the remaining to the right. As he set off, she signaled to Sergeant First-Class Bobby Danials—AKA Bobby Bullets, an expert sharpshooter who kept a lookout no more than forty feet from the tunnel entrance, peering through his rifle scope, the team's eye in the sky.

She signaled him to take out the POWs hanging by hooks in the middle of the camp in approximately twelve minutes. Tapping one forefinger to her head, she directed him to administer a single shot to each POW.

Flaker hustled into her first hut and stopped in the doorway, taken back by the horror in front of her. She couldn't believe the men were alive after all these years, considering the shape they were in—amputated body parts, deep open wounds. Their bodies were skeletons wrapped in a thin layer of skin.

Thirteen men lined the floor, some overlapping each other within the tight quarters. The room smelled like a sewer, and their moaning seemed to bounce off the mildewed walls.

Flaker hushed them gently, fearing her team's presence would be noticed.

She approached one of the POWs and stared down at him. Lying on an old weather-beaten wooden plank, a solder with a long gray beard stared at her as though seeing a mirage.

Flaker touched the man's face and he reached for her hand, giving her a toothless grin.

"I knew you'd come for us! Goddamn, I just knew it!" Then he noticed what Flaker carried in her right hand—a cocked, automatic, silenced handgun.

He looked back into her face. "I understand." He reached under his bedding and handed her a small bottle wrapped in a dirty piece of cloth.

"That's my blood. There's more going on here than you know. Do what you will with me, but if your superiors let you out of this jungle alive, analyze that blood and you'll see the full picture. Keep an open mind."

Flaker wiped away her tears. "Your courage won't be in vain, I promise you."

She lifted her gun to his forehead, and a hollow thump sounded as she pulled the trigger.

* * *

Gecko Bravo Headquarters - 1020

Back at the Gecko Bravo Branch, at communications, Greg Numan stood by the monitoring console, breathing down the console operator's neck.

"Sir," the operator said, "it looks like the mission teams are moving away from their current position."

The console bleeped and the screen abruptly went blank.

Numan leaned in. "What in the fuck is going on?"

"I don't know, sir. It looks like we've lost them."

"How is that possible?"

"Let me see if I can reroute the connection."

Numan picked up the telephone and patched a line through to Walker. "Sir, we've lost the mission team on the monitor."

"Shit!" Walker slammed down the phone.

Moments later, he appeared at Numan's side. "How long since we lost the tracking?"

"Five minutes, sir!"

"That's about four minutes too long, you fuck." He pulled Numan aside and leaned in close, his breath stinking of cigarettes. "If I continue to feel you're attempting to fuck me in this objective, I'm going to kill you, mail your body parts to Washington, and ask kindly for a replacement. I hope I'm being clear?"

The government man could only nod in response.

"Fantastic. Get our translator and have him meet me in my office, immediately."

12

"Four, three, two, one."

From his distant perch, Bobby Bullets eliminated the hanging POWs and scanned the area. His job from there was to make sure their exit was flawless.

Flaker signaled for the teams to rally as she and Buckner hurried toward the exit point. The team ran for the tunnel. She called to Bobby Bullets. "We're clearing out of here, soldier. Get your ass moving."

Still on lookout for any sign of a tail, Bobby shuffled into the tunnel, leaving Flaker behind as he double-timed it back through the maze of tunnels that connected the prison camp to their push-off point.

She paused at the opening of the tunnel, leveled her weapon at the main communications box and fired three neat shots. Then, she entered the tunnel and set off a duster to seal the opening behind her.

After a four-mile scramble through the underground maze, the teams arrived back to the base of the war holes. Flaker was close behind.

Buckner shouted, "I advise you all to get your second wind—we move out in less than five."

Flaker held up one hand to get the group's attention. "Team, this is highly unorthodox, but I ask you to hear me out. On our way out of the camp, I destroyed our main communications box. I believe that certain factions in the United States were using it as a tracking device. We have approximately thirty-four minutes to make rendezvous, but there's a problem with those orders."

She paused as the soldiers exchanged puzzled looks.

"There won't be a chopper waiting for us. In fact, the architects of this operation intend to have us killed."

"Bullshit," Buckner said, stepping in front of her. "I'm pulling you out of this. Consider your command relieved." He turned to the group. "We'll carry out our objective as scheduled."

Ghost stepped up. "If Captain Flaker is removed, I hold command over this regiment of Rangers. As such, I need to know why she's being relieved."

"We haven't got time for explanations, soldier. We have less than thirty minutes to make it to our rendezvous and set off our explosives. As commanding officer of this operation, I order you to move out. Failure to do so will make you subject to court martial. Do I make myself clear, soldier?"

Flaker kept her eyes trained to the ground, jaw set but silent. Ghost reluctantly saluted Buckner. "Yes, sir!" He turned to his team. "Rangers, we will make rendezvous under the command of Lieutenant Buckner. Understood?"

"Hooah!"

Buckner took a step towards Flaker. "Captain," he said. "If you feel strongly in your convictions, we'll send an away team back for you once we return to the United States. If not, you're welcome to make rendezvous with the rest of us."

SEAL 12 raised his eyes from his satellite surveillance laptop. "Captain, just so you know, we're not registering any local threats, either air or surface. Satellite surveillance shows absolutely nothing within our perimeter. The coordinates I just assessed were approximately a three-mile radius. In addition, we're not reading any heightened activity on any of the local lines."

Buckner nodded. "Mission teams, move out."

Flaker touched his arm. "You don't understand what's going on here. Our lives are in danger."

He ignored her, climbing out of the burrow behind the teams.

She watched them go, the jungle seeming to close in behind. After a moment, she sighed and followed. This was the first time in her career she had questioned an order. If she were wrong, she'd be court-martialed and face a ruined career. If she were right, her team would die. Either way, it was a losing game. Her only hope was to stay close to the team and keep them safe.

* * *

Post Base 22-987 Dingo - 1033

Agent Doug Ingro flashed his clearance badge to Thimpkin's secretary.

"I need to speak with General Thimpkin immediately."

The secretary frowned. "I'm sorry, sir, he left about thirty minutes ago for Washington, but he—"

Ingro rushed to Thimpkin's door, kicked it in, and began rummaging through the papers on his desk. "Sir!" the secretary—Ingro noticed she was a pretty young private with ANDREWS on her lapel—rushed in after him. "You're not allowed in here."

Ingro turned. "You have no idea of what I can or can't do. Where the fuck is Thimpkin?"

She leveled her sidearm at the intruder. "I advise you to leave this office. I will put you down, sir."

"You ever shot anyone, Private?" Ingro smirked at her.

"I've had plenty of target practice." She pushed her glasses up with a shaking hand before returning it to the weapon. "Agent, if it comes to it I'll blow your fucking head clean off your shoulders and reserve that ugly eye patch of yours as my new paperweight. *Sir.*"

He held his hands up for a moment, smirking playfully before brushing past her on his way out. "Bitch."

On his way back to the helicopter, Ingro contacted Walker.

"Sir, we've lost him. His secretary said he's on his way to Washington. She's lying through her fucking teeth."

There was a brief, deadly pause. "Just get back here," Walker responded, disconnecting.

* * *

Thanh Pho Ho Chi Minh - 1132

Thimpkin and his rescue squad soared through the sky en route to the rendezvous. They cut low to the thick trees, avoiding radar, the twin Sikorsky Pave Hawks burning through the miles.

"Sergeant Mirrors, what's our ETA, soldier?" Thimpkin spoke into his headphones.

After a brief glance at his area mapping system, then a look out the front window at the landscape, the pilot glanced at Thimpkin. "This can't be right. The mapping system shows our latitude is 10.78 degrees north and our longitude to be 106.69 degrees east. Sir, we're already in Vietnam on the outskirts of the city Thanh Pho Ho Chi Minh. General, according to the readout, we should make the rendezvous site in approximately thirty minutes."

Thimpkin readied his weapon. "We're exactly where we should be by this time, given the unique technology we have at our disposal."

"What are you—"

"That is classified, Sergeant. Pilot the chopper and mind your own business."

"Yes, sir." Mirrors focused on the instrument panel.

Thimpkin felt the silence grow between them. "Am I correct that you got your flight training with the Wicked-Winged-96 at Pensacola?"

"That is correct, sir."

"The W.W.96. Hot damn! Them boys are no joke."

"Damn right, General!" They flew in silence for another minute. "Sir, if you don't mind me asking, why did you choose me for this operation? I've been on the shit list since Guatemala."

"You did an outstanding job for us in Operation Black Bumble."

"With all due respect, General, I don't know what the hell you're talking about."

"My apologies, Sergeant. Your mission under Operation Sweep was to drop off Lieutenant Colonel Divan Marquette and his four-man security team with hostile Guatemalan refugees. You emerged as the sole survivor of the heavy Guatemalan attack. Your contact was Agent Damion Walker of the National Security Agency. Somehow, you made it back to the carrier ship with your flank propeller immobilized. Once again I have to place you in harm's way, but you should know that when we return, your record will be expunged and the pending investigation of your actions will be closed."

"Thank you, sir," Mirrors said.

Thimpkin stared out the window, thinking about the excellent pilot beside him. He knew Mirrors wanted to be part of Special Cavalry Services Black Ops. He also knew that the man was on Fierce Chicanery's primary hit list. Mirrors knew nothing of the plot against his life, not only for his part in the planned assassination of a United States colonel, but for the assassination of a member of Fierce Chicanery.

The murdered Colonel Marquette had been undercover at the time of Operation Black Bumble, working on an ongoing operation for Fierce Chicanery. Thimpkin suspected that Walker's involvement had something to do with Project Aneman or some other secret program in which Special Cavalry Services Black Ops was immersed. However, Thimpkin couldn't figure out how Fierce Chicanery had been in the dark regarding the plot on Colonel Marquette's life.

* * *

Southern Vietnamese Plains - 1143

Under Lieutenant Buckner's leadership, the mission team double-timed it through the southern plains, moving in unison like a sweeper team. Time was too short to establish a defensive perimeter. They humped south with a quickness, knowing they needed to arrive in time to indicate their position to the choppers. Since Flaker had destroyed their primary command communicator, they were traveling in the dark.

Flaker followed fifty feet behind the group, keeping the team in sight while she performed a hasty solo perimeter lookout.

Buckner brought the team to an abrupt halt by holding one fist aloft. The soldiers instantly dropped to the dirt. Following their lead, Buckner placed one ear to the ground. A rumbling sound suggested movements from individuals or a convoy. He motioned SEAL 12 closer with the satellite surveillance unit.

"Double-time it on that readout," Buckner said.

"It should be up within thirty seconds, sir." Flaker saw the team stop and checked the brush through her binoculars. She spotted some unusual action off to the right of the southern trail.

After moving to a different vantage point, she saw the Vietnamese soldiers set up in ambush formation on either side of the team.

At the same instant, SEAL 12's satellite surveillance came on line, indicating they were surrounded by hundreds of unknowns.

"Fuck me." Buckner said. "It's about to get hotter in this kitchen."

The team readied their weapons. Among them, Ghost's typically inscrutable face belied his anger and disappointment.

"Lieutenant," SEAL 12 whispered.

"What the fuck is it?" Buckner crawled back to his position.

SEAL 12 spun his laptop around so Buckner could see the screen. "We're fucked, sir."

They were lying on a hotbed of explosives wired at least six feet beneath their location and stretching thirty feet on either side.

"Ambush!" Buckner shouted.

Flaker heard the distant call from her location. She cocked her semiautomatic weapon, but it was too late; she watched helplessly as her team was destroyed. A series of fierce explosions sent the team flying. Most were killed instantly by the impact, their limbs torn off. Flaker rose to see a conflagration of shrapnel, smoke, and dust before her. She ran to the site, using the smoke and dust as cover. Moving from soldier to soldier in search of survivors, she heard the Vietcong soldiers approach.

One of the Vietcong soldiers shouted. Gunfire cut the air.

Flaker fired back, still watching her feet. She spotted Buckner, limbs intact, knocked out cold. She removed the explosive detonator from his pocket, flipped the detonator's trigger and set off a series of explosives back at the Vietnamese prison camp. Explosions ripped through the camp, catching the remaining Vietcong off-guard.

Hefting Buckner onto her shoulders, Flaker ran for the rendezvous site. The Vietcong fire became sporadic; they assumed they were up against an entire team of Americans scattered throughout the bush.

A hot Vietcong AK pistol round tore through Flaker's shoulder and she fell to the ground. The pain sent her adrenaline pumping. She tried to get back up and continue fighting, but Buckner's body weighed heavy on her and she fell back, pinned. A Vietcong caught up with her.

"I've got the filthy Westerner!" he shouted, standing over her. When he realized he'd captured a woman, his smile turned into a leer—a look Flaker knew all too well.

Flaker stared into the man's eyes as he took a quick moment to wipe his forehead. Before she could make another move, Ghost approached with his knife and attacked the soldier, stroking his knife deep across the man's neck. Bright blood oozed.

There wasn't much time before the Vietcong would close in. Ghost helped Flaker to her feet, lifted Buckner and tore out of the field. Flaker limped behind, covering with gunfire and grenades. Low on ammo, she spun her AK-47 around to her back and pulled her double-action .40 Smith & Wesson cartridge, Heckler and Koch P7 M13. It wasn't exactly a military-issue weapon, but it was a favorite and served as a bit of a good luck charm.

"If we can make it to that wooded sector, maybe we'll have a chance," she shouted. A series of explosions went off around them. They heard the steady beat of approaching helicopters.

Mounted machine guns lit the sky with streaks of fire. Two heavily armed Pave Hawk helicopters burst through the swirl of jungle dew and misty smoke. General George Thimpkin leaned out from one, watching the other land. To Flaker, the sight of him resembled a gray ghost swooping in from Valhalla with an arsenal forged by the hands of the gods. The soldiers ran for the chopper, the unconscious Buckner still draped over Ghost's broad shoulders. Flaker made sure the others were safe, then held her arms up toward Thimpkin's chopper to give the all clear.

A missile struck Thimpkin's chopper, destroying it instantly.

* * *

Flaker's adrenaline pounded in the rising chopper. She was alert of every movement made by the pilot and the shooter. Once they were clear, she pulled her sidearm, pushed the shooter toward the front with the pilot, and placed her pistol on the pilot's temple. The pilot's head jerked when the hot barrel touched him. It all happened too fast to think and if the men had a complaint, they didn't voice it. "Name and rank?" she shouted at the pilot.

"Sergeant Major Harold Holang," said the pilot.

Leveling her gun on the shooter: "And you?"

"Second Lieutenant David Thousin."

She sat back, her gun still raised. "What's your business in this mission?"

"We received orders from General Thimpkin to rendezvous with you at the Southern Vietnamese Plains and to drop you off in a secured location," Thousin said. He paused for a moment to look down at Captain Flaker's gun, then back at the pilot. "If you check behind you, you'll see a package. General Thimpkin noted that if anything happened to him, you were to receive it."

Lowering her gun, Flaker reached behind her and found a metal case equipped with a digital combination lock. An engraving on top of the case read:

What was the dastardly deed on a night five and seventeen broke free, before the death of greed?

It was a riddle which could only be answered by two people: Kalista and her brother Reggie. The code referred to events that happened the night before her mother and father died. She entered the code one letter at a time and heard a subtle buzzing after each entry: R—A—P—E—before the case popped open with a click. She glanced at its contents, her full attention still on the shooter and the pilot.

She closed the case and stared out the chopper door. Now that the firing had stopped, it was easy to say goodbye to the peaceful land of imprisoned ghosts.

In a clearing ahead, a black Expedition sat on a trail, camping gear harnessed to the top. She watched two black Hummers spin off into the brush. She held her weapon close.

Once Flaker and her comrades had cleared the chopper, it lifted gracefully in the air again, beginning its slow climb. Ghost was already loading Lieutenant Buckner into the car. Flaker stood her ground, watching the helicopter pull away from the jungle.

"To hell with this mission!" she shouted after it, her words lost in the noise. She knew one thing: the mission wasn't over yet.

13

It was a dark, rainy morning. Kalista stood alone on a running path by a stand that usually sold umbrellas and sunglasses; closed now, at four in the morning. She wore all black, long pants and a sweatshirt with the hood up. Her eyes caught the soft glow of a nearby street lamp.

Was it worth it?

Were the lives of her team worth it? Was her career worth it? The three survivors of the mission vanished after they returned stateside. Ghost took a train into Mexico, never to be heard from again. And before he died, General Thimpkin gave Kalista a gift that would keep on giving, financing her freedom. How she had loved that man.

Kalista sometimes found herself fantasizing that the Vietcong had killed her outright in that jungle; she deserved to die with her soldiers for what she'd done.

As she stretched for the ten miles ahead, Kalista tried not to think about the sad state of her life. She was doomed to solitude, watching life pass by, tormented by the absolute knowledge that evil was still running wild. Thimpkin taught her to be a person of strength and integrity—a woman with the heart of a lioness—yet here she was, years later, hiding out like a common criminal.

As the five-year anniversary of her mission in Vietnam rolled past, Kalista had celebrated by meditating on the bastards who killed Thimpkin and her team. She wanted revenge for being stripped of the career she'd worked so hard to achieve, revenge for the deaths that plagued her life, revenge for her destroyed faith in the goodness of life, America, and the government. Destroying the conspirators would stop their reign of terror over her country and the world.

As she escaped the Vietnamese plains that bloody morning, for the first time in her career she couldn't project where she'd be the next day. She couldn't imagine how she would live, how she could start her life over. All she knew was that unknowns within the United States government had initiated the top secret operation that changed her life.

For years afterward she mourned her men, the POWs they killed that day, and her friend, the general. Time passed in darkness. It wasn't until September 11, 2001, that she finally understood. During the three years after the 1998 mission, Kalista slowly, quietly updated her at-home lab facility. What had started as a few vials in her den was steadily becoming a complete do-it-yourself testing facility. When chaos fell the city on September 11, she headed straight to her lab and unlocked the vial she'd received from the Vietnam vet during the mission. The blood was still intact—tainted, no doubt, by its time in the jungle, but hopefully usable. It would take years to finish quietly gathering the materials to test it, but until then, she kept the sample in cold storage.

For years, the Vietnamese government bragged about what it had done that day. The soldiers who died so bravely were thrown away, and their families received no explanation from the government. Instead of dying heroes to the Corps, they were forgotten. The Vietnamese government allowed their soldiers to parade the battered bodies through the streets and the whole thing was shown on national television, proving to the world that the United States had covertly been in their territory for one reason or another.

Kalista could hardly believe the cruelty of her country, but she had witnessed it with her own eyes. The first year of military withdrawal was as painful as the thirteen bullet wounds she'd taken throughout her career.

Rounding the corner in her final stretch of the ten-mile course, she set off for home. All of the equipment was installed and she was finally prepared to begin.

Part II

The Shroud Unravels

14

In the five years since that fateful day in the southern Vietnamese plains, Riondro Buckner lay in a comatose state in Kalista's spare bedroom.

"Another day, huh?" she said cheerily, checking his feeding tube. An ICU worth of medical tools and monitoring devices surrounded the prone soldier. "You keep dreaming, because it's no better on this end, trust me."

She sat on the bed and touched his hand. "Riondro," she whispered, "you've got to wake up. Put your foot on the gas, soldier, and get on your fucking feet."

Riondro's eyelids twitched. She held her breath for a second, but it was just a reflex.

She sighed and stood. "Rest while you can, Lieutenant. We have a lot to do when you wake up."

* * *

Hanna Jenkins pulled into Kalista's driveway and knocked on the front door. The licensed practical nurse carried a medical bag.

Inside, Kalista had been snacking on an apple at the table when she heard the knock. She readied her favorite double-action

Heckler & Koch from the kitchen cupboard where she stored it among the canned goods. Still chewing, she trained her weapon toward the door.

"Who is it?"

A gentle voice returned. "It's Hanna."

Kalista picked up the apple and tucked the gun into her waistband, where it was easily concealed under her baggy button-down.

"Prove it!" Kalista said.

"Open this door or I'll turn you over my knee," Hanna returned.

Grinning, Kalista undid a series of locks and swung the door open. "What's up, girlfriend?"

"Hi, sweetie." Hanna brushed by her with a quick hug. "How's everything?"

"Same as always. I'll be in the den if you need me."

Upstairs, Hanna sat at the desk in the bedroom with her back to Riondro, filling out her paperwork while singing the tune from Cheers.

Taking a break from the world today takes everything you've got —
Taking a break from all your worries sure does help a lot —
Wouldn't you like to get away—

Behind her, Riondro moved his legs.

Hanna stared out the window, calculating her take-home pay for the week. This was a cushy job and she expected to retire from it, because she'd never yet seen a patient recover after five years in a coma. Kalista paid her extremely well, and she was sworn to secrecy about anything that went on inside the house.

A box of tissues fell from the side table attached to the bed. She turned around quickly, startled, noticing the box on the floor.

Her patient was quiet, with no sign of movement. She pulled the sheet over his shoulders.

"Of all the strange things—"

As if he had awakened from a brief nap, Riondro Buckner raised his head, eyes wide.

Hanna screamed at the top of her lungs.

Within a matter of seconds, Kalista burst into the room, maneuvering a tuck and roll, coming up with her weapon drawn.

Hanna shrank back. "Don't shoot me!"

Kalista paused in disbelief when she spotted Riondro's confused gaze. "Holy shit, you're awake!" she whispered under her breath.

Hanna sank into a chair, fanning herself with a magazine. "Lord, you scared the bejesus out of me."

* * *

For the next ten days, Riondro drifted in and out of a restless sleep. He would talk of his sons, of Sharon, and of his father and his mother. The strange woman was always there, without the gun this time, putting a cool cloth on his forehead, bathing him, calming him. He came to see her as an angel who lingered over him at night. Sometimes she simply sat and held his hand, brushing his hair. Telling him everything was okay.

Near the end of the second week, he broke free from the worst of his agonizing state.

Working the use back into his legs in bed, he watched the scene out his window, admiring the lush grass and trees.

"Five years?" he muttered. "Five years. Five years."

Kalista tapped on the door then entered, carrying a tray of food. "I thought you might be hungry."

"Thank you." Riondro accepted the tray on his lap. "My legs are like rubber."

She passed him the food and sat in a chair beside the bed. "How are you feeling otherwise?"

He looked hard at her face. "Are you an angel?"

"You don't know who I am?"

It seemed like a trap. He didn't respond.

"Do you know who you are?"

He shrugged. "I feel so lost."

The tray was laden with a sandwich, chips, and a glass of milk. He picked at the food as if he wasn't even sure how to eat it. "I'll help you get through this. Meanwhile, call me Kalista. All my friends do."

* * *

That night, Buckner fell into a restless sleep, twitching and squirming in bed, dripping with sweat. In the dream, he drove a utility vehicle through New York, on his way home from Central Park where he'd spent the afternoon with his family. His little boys, Bobby and Trent, played in the back seat. His wife received a page from her office.

"Damn," Sharon said, looking at her pager. "Honey?" She turned to him with a nervous smile.

"All right, I'll swing by your office so you can check on whatever it is you have to check on." He made a quick right turn.

"I mean, since we're downtown," she said.

"Whatever you want, sweetheart," he said. "As long as you're willing to pay for it later."

They laughed. Within a few minutes, he pulled up across the street from the World Trade Center. The boys stopped playing to gaze at the huge buildings, their heads hanging out the side window as they peered upward.

As she got out of the car, she asked the boys, "Trent, Bobby, do you want to come inside with Mommy?" Excited, they piled out of the car, anxious to go up to her office on the eighteenth floor. "Baby, you coming?" she asked Riondro.

"No way am I going to try and find parking. I'll wait for you guys."

"Okay, but I'd better not come back and find you smoking out here." She winked at him. Then, looking both ways, she walked the boys across the street and into the building. He watched them go, then leaned against the car, fished the pack of cigarettes out of his sock and lit one.

As he held the flame to the cigarette, an explosion rocked the area, throwing him off his balance. His head slammed against the concrete, leaving a bloody gash.

When Riondro came to, he saw dozens of people lying on the ground. The building across the street was partially destroyed from the bomb blast. The sirens and screams in the background sounded faint and far away.

"No!" he screamed. He fell to his knees, crying and calling out for his family.

* * *

Riondro woke up to a knock on the door. He swung his legs over the side of the bed, painfully got up and hobbled into the bathroom. "Are you okay in there?" Kalista asked on the other side.

"Just give me a minute," he answered, fighting to keep his composure.

"There's clothing in the closet. When you get ready, come find me downstairs." He heard her footsteps trail down the hall.

"Sharon, Trent, Bobby—who are they?" he asked himself. He opened the closet to find military issue black ops training gear, which he found fit him perfectly. Carefully, testing the weight on his legs, he left the room.

Kalista's place seemed like a well-maintained shell—a lovely house, but not a home. Knockoffs of beautiful framed paintings hung on the walls and the furniture was clean and expensive looking. There was no hint of dust or disorder.

The window frames were metal with reinforced glass. He had examined the windows in his bedroom and discovered they were equipped with some sort of high-tech sensory device. Although the windows were shut, he felt a faint breeze moving through the house, smelling of elements like iron, brick, plastic, and sulfur.

Why did he have the ability to pick up on such things? He didn't know, but felt it necessary to go with the flow—especially if it might help him regain his memory. More than anything, he wanted to know who he was.

Downstairs in the front hallway, he stopped to look around. The hall opened into an empty living room.

As he stood in the doorway, something grabbed him from behind. A kick to his lower back flung him forward and he hit the wall. He quickly regained his balance and looked around, but nobody was in sight. Within seconds he was attacked again, this time from the side. The attacker charged him, swinging and striking him in the face, causing him to bleed from his nose. The attacker gave a kick to the ribs and then to his right leg, causing him to fall to his knees.

He shook his head, seeing the attacker take a step before kicking him directly in the face. He fell backwards, his head slamming against the wooden floor. His assailant stood above him in hooded black gear, shaking his head. The hooded figure turned away from him and walked off.

Seeing the attacker turn away, Riondro leapt to his feet with strength he didn't know he possessed.

"Don't I get a chance to earn my money back?" he asked, wiping the blood from his face.

The attacker turned to face him. Their eyes locked in a standoff. This time Riondro struck first. He dropped to one knee and strategically buckled his attacker's knees. Riondro administered a swift upper cut, connecting his fist with the attacker's lower jaw. This sent his opponent flying, landing dazed on the floor.

He began another advance when the attacker whipped off his mask.

It was his angel, the woman of his dreams—Kalista Flaker. She stood before him, grinning. "Okay, okay, I give up." She held out her hands.

"Why the hell did you just try and kill me?"

"You asked me to help you," Kalista said. "I needed to know if you'd react like you're trained to react. Though it took some time, you passed with flying colors. I think you're still the badass I used to know."

"What training?" Riondro asked.

"Be patient. You'll soon know everything there is to know about yourself, your past, your future, and then some. Who you are is vital to me." She peeled off her gloves. "I need you all there before we push on. You, Riondro Buckner, are a vital part of the future of this country and the world."

He stared at her, rubbing his shoulder.

"But you got me a little riled up," she said. "I haven't had live contact in years—five years, to be exact."

"Where did I learn this stuff?"

"Let's go to the gym and spar while you're warmed up. I'll explain as we go." She led him through the kitchen and down another set of stairs to a fully equipped gym with state-of-the-art weight equipment, sparring material, and even a shooting range.

She tested a punching bag on a thick chain. "You're trained in practically all areas of fighting, including martial arts, combat, survival, and instant death maneuvers," she said. "That's why I stopped you when I did. But now we need to practice."

"I don't fight women."

She laughed. "In the future, we might find ourselves in a situation where you can't look at me as a woman. While we're training, don't throw that bullshit conditioned sexist sympathy in; it might get us both killed. Enough. Let's begin."

She threw a kick at him and they began fighting. Though he was hesitant at first, Riondro quickly realized Kalista was his equal. What she didn't possess in brute strength, she made up for in quickness and guile. After fifteen minutes they called a truce. He clutched his side and her lip was bleeding.

"Good," she panted, "you're getting there. But I still think you're holding back on me. Don't get comfortable. We aren't through yet!"

He was shocked at her stamina, and also his own. Somewhere between the bedroom and the hallway, he'd found the strength to use his body in extraordinary ways even after years of disuse.

She attacked, swinging at his face. He maneuvered her to the ground in a position she couldn't seem to break. As she struggled beneath him, everything momentarily went black. He saw himself on the Vietnamese plains, then a massive explosion went off around him and his body flew through the air.

"Hold on, Lieutenant, I'm going to get you out of here," Kalista said. That was the last thing he remembered.

He was still pinning her to the mat when he came back to reality. At once he reeled back against the wall, holding both his hands over his eyes.

"What is it?" she asked, getting to her feet.

"You saved my life! There was an explosion and I was hurt. You came and pulled me out. After that, everything went black."

She smiled. "It's coming back to you, Riondro, one piece at a time. It's coming back!"

15

A pearl black stretch limousine drove down a barren stretch of desert road, led by one black Hummer and trailed by a second. The vehicle's passengers were Agent Damion Walker, Agent Doug Ingro, and Dr. Harold Grog, a test scientist at the secret underground facility in Arizona known as Unit 87.

This vast stretch of desert was known as Chicciihie Point, a sacred Indian burial ground until Western civilization staked claim to the lands. They were more than eighty miles outside Phoenix, isolated from the civilized world.

Walker stared through tinted windows at the barren landscape. "You'd better have good news," he muttered.

Dr. Grog spoke up. "Sir, we've made some drastic breakthroughs at the unit. I'm sure you'll be pleased."

The lead Hummer parked in front of a mound of dirt. A group of men in black piled out of the lead and tail cars and quickly scouted the perimeter. One of them tapped on the limousine window. "Sir, everything's clear."

The three men exited the vehicle. Tapping on a remote attached to his wrist, Dr. Grog punched in a code. The ground beneath them began to hum and within seconds, dirt blew away from the mound, revealing a flat metal panel about half a mile long and half a mile wide. Walker, Ingro, and their security team followed the scientist onto the surface, which contained a number of body-length circular disks.

"Gentlemen, if you will, step on one of the circles, keep your hands close to your body, and stay absolutely still." Dr. Grog adjusted his thick bifocals and took the lead.

Once the men were in place, the humming sound began again and the circles descended into the earth.

The men found themselves inside a chamber connected to a long, brightly lit white tunnel. The eight bodyguards led, followed by Ingro and Walker. Dr. Grog brought up the rear, carrying a clipboard he'd pulled off the wall as he entered the facility.

"Gentlemen, when we first obtained and tested the serum, we had no idea what long-term effects it would have on our soldiers. That's why it didn't," he turned the page on his clipboard, "work. But now we've discovered the extraterrestrial DNA mutated as it died, breaking down the anatomy of the living host, in an attempt to remain alive as an untainted neutral entity—"

Walker interrupted. "So you're saying it took years to discover this shit was occurring in how many of my soldiers?"

"Ninety-eight over a period of four years, sir." Walker attacked the scientist with a pressure maneuver to the side of his throat, causing him to drop to his knees.

"Fuck what you're saying and fuck you," he growled. "If this shit's not correct this time, I'm going to split you in half and watch you slowly die." He slowly increased the pressure on Dr. Grog's carotid artery. "Ninety-eight of my men were sacrificed while you and your team of idiots guessed your way through this whole process."

"Sir, you're hurting me!" Dr. Grog cried, squirming.

"Pick him up." Walker let go and the man dropped to his hands and knees. Ingro pulled Grog to his feet.

"Sir," the scientist said, gasping for air. "We didn't know the extraterrestrial DNA's survival strategy was to remain subservient. In layman's terms, the DNA played dead. Now we've rectified the situation by melting the organism, then mixing it with the DNA of forty-nine species of animals and reptiles." They reached a large door that slowly opened at their approach. "Those species featured had close DNA strands and other biomedical similarities to the alien DNA. We then mixed this with human DNA to create the long-awaited Aneman, which strengthens all senses and quadruples the strength of the injected party. To give it to you straight, sir? We did it."

"Show me," Walker said.

Donning surgical masks and gowns, they entered the laboratory. Inside, seven glass-enclosed capsules sat along the wall. Each capsule contained a single man, naked and apparently asleep. Ten men and six women dressed in scrubs bustled around the room, monitoring vital signs and running lab tests on urine and blood from the subjects.

"Are all these men Anemen?" Walker asked.

"Two of the seven have gone through the testing phase. The rest have been injected, but in this state it takes a while for the serum to become effective. If they're disturbed in this state, we could risk killing them."

Walker paced the floor, looking at the men. "Well, thaw the two out and give me a demonstration. I want to see them in action."

* * *

Dr. Grog led the way to a viewing room above a large atrium. Below, a silent group of scientists strapped sensory devices onto the prone bodies.

"What's wrong with them?" Walker asked. "They seem too quiet, like they're in a trance."

"They're completely focused, sir, obedient in every way." Dr. Grog said with a smile. "They want to please you in this demonstration, just as I do."

"Tell us what we're looking at," Walker said.

"We mastered mind control some thirty years ago, sir. These Anemen proved to be perfect candidates for that project and I took the initiative and decided to fuse that technology with the Aneman objective. With the Aneman serum thoroughly synthesized and administered, the only other step to achieve mind control was to inject our serum directly into the temporal lobe of the candidates." Dr. Grog waved the scientists out of the demonstration room. "Mr. Walker," he said. "What we've achieved is nothing short of the perfect soldier."

"A new world order," Walker said, watching the men standing alone in the center of the atrium.

"The sky's the limit."

A doorway opened in the atrium and a huge black bear entered, observing its surroundings for only a moment before charging the men at full speed.

Dr. Grog smiled as everyone's jaw dropped. "Not exactly Smokey, is he? That bear is infested with a tweaked form of rabies. We call it Viral 8. The animal feels no pain and has only one objective."

"And what's that?" Walker asked, his eyes fixed on the demonstration.

"Killing everything in the room, sir."

The two Anemen stand their ground, unafraid. When the bear was near enough, each took a firm grip on the animal's front paws, oblivious to the huge claws. Within seconds, they ripped the bear's arms from their sockets and the animal dropped abruptly to the ground, roaring, fighting to get up. The Anemen turned to the viewing window with matching salutes.

Grog checked his watch. "Exactly nineteen seconds."

"Impressive."

Pointing to the monitor, Dr. Grog said, "If you'll check this readout, gentlemen, you'll see their heart rate barely increased and they only used twelve percent of their strength to take the animal down. Next, we'll see them in hand-to-hand."

He raised his arm to the operator's room. Instantly, two massive gorillas charged into the room, bloody foam seeping from their mouths.

"Watch closely," Dr. Grog said. He seemed to be foaming a little at the mouth, himself. He spoke into the intercom. "Gentlemen, you have ten seconds to eliminate your targets."

"Yes, sir!" the Anemen shouted in unison.

Each man charged a gorilla, slamming against it like a bullet and tackling it to the ground. Moving in perfect unison, they each quickly straddled the beasts and snapped their necks. The gorillas didn't stand a chance.

Again, they saluted the viewing window.

"That was unbelievable," Walker said. "I want to see more. Strength, brute force, obedience, and speed are one thing. I want to see strategy, smarts, tactical capabilities, and combat scenarios."

The scientist waved a hand. "The tests you've mentioned have been documented thoroughly and show our candidates have skill levels that far surpass America's most skilled Special Forces. In addition, we enhanced their IQs to the genius range. In my opinion, these Anemen could lead brilliant, unstoppable armies in any combat situation. They could protect presidents or become presidents."

Dr. Grog handed Walker a sealed case. "Enclosed you'll find documentation—including videos, combat simulations, plus our mind-control schematics."

Walker smirked at the briefcase and tossed it to Ingro. "You've impressed me, Doctor."

"I've got one more surprise for you. Through gene manipulation on the structural level, we have also made it possible for these men to procreate. The Anemen have become a self-sustaining race."

* * *

Fifteen minutes later, standing before the Anemen in a sealed laboratory, Walker favored Dr. Grog with a rare smile.

"Very good, Doctor. Very, very good. How long does it take for the serum to take effect?"

"Once injected, the serum takes full effect in about forty-eight hours, depending on the subject's metabolism, health, and mental state. We allow the serum to sit for seventy-two hours to make sure nothing goes wrong." The scientist searched through his desk drawers. "After we tested the serum on one of our soldiers, he appeared to have a certain miraculous ability. Ah, here it is."

He stepped forward, holding a handgun pointed at the floor. The security detail rushed in front of Walker and Ingro, guns drawn. The scientist swung around and shot one of the Anemen in the left thigh. The man fell to the floor, yelping in pain.

Walker rushed forward, furious. "Are you out of your fucking mind?"

Before he finished the sentence, the Aneman stood, unsteady at first, and then walked without pain to his comrade. He saluted the stunned group.

The scientist ticked open the pant leg with a pen, showing the assembled group that the wound had completely healed without even a scar. The security detail lowered their guns, shocked.

"Not bad," the scientist said, obviously pleased with himself. "With the drastic change in their DNA structure, their immune systems can rebuild body tissues thousands of times faster than normal. As for the bullet—it will be broken down by the soldier's blood. The acid content in the Aneman's blood can penetrate and dissolve anything it comes in contact with."

"Impressive indeed," Walker said. "Round up your staff. I want to congratulate them myself."

"Of course." Dr. Grog hurried off down the hallway.

"Sir—" Ingro began.

"As discussed," Walker confirmed, sizing up the silent Anemen.

* * *

Thirty minutes later, Dr. Grog's team filed into a conference room and seated themselves around the table to face Walker, Ingro, and their security. The security team spread out across the room, with two remaining beside the door.

The scientists chatted nervously as Dr. Grog hurried to the front of the room. "People, I'd like to introduce Agent Damion Walker from the Department of National Security. As our employer for the Aneman project, he deserves our warmest welcome."

Walker and Ingro smirked at each other as the scientists applauded. Dr. Grog signaled Walker to take his place at the front of the conference room.

Walker held his hands out to quiet the group. He scanned the room for his undercover agent and found her by the door. "Tracy Tips?" he called out. "Did you obtain the serum and all necessary digital information?"

The scientists looked at Tips, then at each other.

"Yes, sir," she said, accepting an automatic weapon from one of the security men.

Walker pulled lit a cigarette and took a long, slow drag.

"You're not supposed to—" Dr. Grok began.

"Folks," Walker said. "I can't say it's been great working with you, so I'll just say goodbye." He nodded to the security team. "Eliminate them."

He ducked out through the swinging doors, leaving the screams and gunfire behind. He strolled down the hallway, enjoying his cigarette.

After a few minutes, Ingro met Walker in the hallway. Walker's point man picked flesh and bone from his uniform. "Mission accomplished, sir."

"You have an hour to get this place in order," Walker said. "And get yourself cleaned up. I won't have that filth inside my limousine."

"Of course, sir."

An hour later, as the caravan left the facility, a blinding flash glittered behind them, followed by a sharp explosive sound that shook the ground for miles.

16

Kalista and Riondro sat at the kitchen table, drinking wine and snacking from a tray of cheese and crackers she'd put together. During the past few months they'd become comfortable with each other, which was exactly what she wanted. She'd needed to gain his confidence so he'd trust her in any situation. And she in turn wanted to know him better.

Halfway through their second bottle of Chardonnay, their laughter began winding down. He took a slow sip of wine and watched her spread goat cheese on a cracker.

"You've told me a lot about what happened during the mission," he said, "but what about before? What's my history?"

She took a bite. "I've been giving you bits and pieces of information in the hopes you'd start to remember things on your own. Take it easy, man—it's only been six months since you came out of the coma. Now, your training is complete and your health is back full strength. Your memory will be the last thing to return. Soon, we'll have to push on."

"With a mission?"

She stood and gathered the dishes, heading for the sink. "Things aren't as they appear. Have you ever asked yourself why we've never left this compound?"

"Sure, I've been going stir-crazy. I thought this was all a part of my training."

"It was. And now, we have to take the next step."

"Anything to get out here."

She nodded curtly. "We're dealing with a plan for global rule, starting with our own government. It's chicanery."

"Chicanery," he repeated.

"An evil plot, a conspiracy. People have always speculated that we're not alone, and the things I've discovered add credence to that speculation." She held up a hand against his dubious look. "There was an incident many years ago in Roswell, where supposedly a thunderstorm caused an unidentified flying object and its extraterrestrial occupants to crash. Now, of course, our government covered it up. But apparently, the government has been fooling around with DNA from the aliens they discovered dead at the crash site. Meanwhile, I've been studying a sample I got from one of the Vietnam veterans we eliminated on our last mission."

Riondro rubbed his eyes. Behind them, he saw flashes of the fallen soldiers.

She continued, watching him. "What I found shocked me. Come with me."

At first, Riondro thought he'd had too much to drink as he followed her through the house. Surely he was imagining the corridors she led him through. She walked them down a concrete-lined staircase.. He picked up the scent of raw materials, iron and sulfur. He also sensed that someone else was nearby.

Kalista punched a module on the back of her watch, opening a hidden iron doorway. They stepped into an area resembling a rusted sewage pipeline, then walked thirty feet to a rusty door. The door slid back to reveal yet another door—silver, with a code module off to the side. Again, she entered a code, which opened the door to reveal a laboratory filled with computer equipment, lab chemicals, weapons, and gear. He followed her inside.

The door led them out onto the first floor where the ground was made of tight iron mesh. On the second floor, Riondro saw a young man front of a bank of computers, completely enthralled by the glowing screens. He sported a strange pair of glasses attached to the bank of computers on either side, like they were a part of the computers themselves. Attached to the glasses were foil antennas that towered a foot over his head.

He wore '70s kicks, '80s-style tight ripped jeans, and an AC/DC T-shirt. He styled on his left ear a dangling silver earring and a tattoo on his left wrist in the design of a bracelet, the wording reading BORN TO BE WILD. His spiked hair swung forward and back as he danced about in his chair.

Kalista looked at the awed expression on Riondro's face. "Quite the place, huh? That strange-looking character is my baby brother—our secret third roommate." She led him to a glass-walled elevator and they ascended to the second level.

"I consider this the safest place on earth," she said as she and Riondro stepped out of the elevator and headed toward Reggie's master control center.

Reggie spun his chair around. "Welcome, Riondro Buckner, to the hell in which I live!"

"Ah, thank you," Riondro said.

"So I meet the highly decorated lieutenant at last. I've heard you were one badass son of a bitch!" Reggie sauntered over and held out a scrawny hand. "Don't worry, big man, I just have to shake the hand of a badass like you. Maybe some of that cool-ass shit will rub off on me. Shit, I thought my sister was cool, but compared to you—"

The two shook hands.

"You can call me Reg if you want. I run this shit here!"

"Stinky, now that you've met Superman, get back to work," Kalista said, smiling at her kid brother.

Reggie leaned in to Riondro. "Man, don't pay attention to her. Let me show you my kingdom's master control."

Riondro stared in awe at the computer equipment and satellite tracking systems, all more advanced than he had ever seen. Even NASA didn't have this stuff.

"So, Reg, what exactly do you do here?" he asked.

"I monitor just about anything that walks, talks, moves, or snoozes. In addition, from here, I can tap into any unit, from the military to the National Security Agency to the FBI, without a trace. I can manipulate any flight hangar or air reinforcement for mission covers. Hell, I can even get you a tank if you need one. Do you need a tank?"

"Reggie," Kalista said. "No tanks today."

The young man shrugged, returned to his chair and typed on a console. "With some fancy hacking, I found out these sons of bitches at Gecko Bravo have been into this shit for years, even before the Vietnam War."

The history of the 1947 Roswell incident, complete with photos, appeared on one of the screens.

"With what we've discovered about this project, it makes you wonder about those four thousand-plus men missing in action during the Vietnam Conflict, doesn't it?"

Riondro nodded. "But what's this shit you're talking about them being into?"

"I hope you're not afraid of monsters, because man, we found some scary ones," Reggie said.

Kalista handed Riondro a folder.

"Anything new?" she asked Reggie.

Focusing his attention back on the console, Reggie unwrapped a piece of bubble gum. "Damion Walker and his band of slugs just blew up the supposedly secret Unit 87 in the Arizona desert."

"Well, Riondro," Kalista said. "It looks like there's work for us to do yet. You up for a late-night rendezvous?"

"Why not?" he smiled, closing the folder.

"Oh, yeah!" Reggie shouted. "Let's rock and roll!"

* * *

Arizona Desert - 10:52 p.m.

A full moon bathed the countryside in pale white light as a black Hummer rolled over the terrain.

Inside, Kalista and Riondro were fully equipped in battle gear. She drove, while he stared out the side window, lost in his own mind.

"Penny for your thoughts?" she asked, glancing over.

"I think you'd need a loan." He smiled at her. "Listen, I want to thank you for everything. I feel like I have a purpose again, and I owe it to you. I owe everything to you, in fact."

Reggie's voice from the console interrupted their conversation. "Hey, you're coming up on point. I'm activating your low sensory lights; that means night goggles, people. Let's rock and roll."

Kalista brought the Hummer to a stop.

"Sit tight," Reggie said. "There seems to be some movement down there."

"Scan for weapons," Riondro said. "Give me a temperature readout and test the grounds for possible radiation or chemical residue."

"You got it."

"Reg, also scan in a three-mile radius?"

"Hell yeah, I got you covered, big man. Sit tight."

"Looks like Lieutenant Buckner just made a guest appearance." Kalista said.

Reggie's voice crackled back onto the radio. "All right, I've got zero radiation levels, some chemical residue from test valves in the lab. Looks like the explosion was a series of non-chemical bombs mounted with C-4—about nine of them. No weapons noted. That three-mile radius you requested is cocked, blocked, and the eagle has his eyes open. You two are cleared. I'll guide you through the complex. Whoever's in there isn't not moving much."

"Hit vision change," Kalista said. They both changed the frequency of their night-vision goggles. "Let's go."

They climbed through the rubble with guns up. Kalista led, while Riondro covered.

She picked her way through a massive tangle of coiled wrought iron and crumbled bricks still smoking from the explosion.

Reggie's voice emerged from their COM pieces. "From what I can tell, there are five unarmed people down there," he said. "They seem to be in the room just on your left."

"Stand fast!" Riondro whispered.

Within seconds, they rushed into the room with guns up, finding heavily burned bodies plus shattered rifle casings. All of the individuals were dead.

In another room, the pair found seven capsules, all but two occupied by scorched and battered bodies.

Amazingly, these men were still alive, although in terrible condition. Their flesh was ripped, skulls caved in, bones broken, and limbs were scattered about the capsule. Their flesh was severely darkened due to the flames that had essentially baked them.

"Reg, are you sure there's no one else in here?" Riondro asked.

"From where I sit, you're in the clear."

Riondro approached one of the capsules. "These must be the monsters your brother was talking about."

From the other side of the lab, Kalista collected vials on the countertops. "There's more going on here. Whatever's keeping these men alive, barely, seems to be rebuilding their genetic make-up."

"You knew about all this?"

"All I know is that since 1947, the NSA has been trying to develop some sort of superhuman soldier. I only had one sample to work with since our mission five years ago. I'm praying this new sample will give me a little more insight into this unethical government objective before it's too late. I'm afraid if they achieve their goal, the world will stand no chance against them."

Riondro was quiet for a moment before he turned to her. "A new world order?" he asked.

"Exactly."

17

"Somebody get Agent Ingro—now!" shouted the console operator at the Gecko Bravo Branch, watching his monitor.

"What is it?" Ingro rushed to the console.

"There's activity at Unit 87, sir."

"We destroyed that place! No one should know about—" he looked at the monitor, narrowing his eyes.

In a moment, Ingro was rushing toward Walker's office. "Sir, we have a problem. Unit 87 has visitors."

"Whoever's down there has nothing to discover. The acid explosion we used to destroy the unit should've wiped away any evidence," Walker said. A cigarette dangled from his mouth as he positioned himself for an invisible tee-off, his nine-iron set to swing. "It's probably just a group of Area 51 type assholes looking for a story." He swung the nine-iron with a smooth follow through, the air around the club whistling. "Just to be on the safe side, get out there and get rid of them."

"Yes, sir."

Walker called after him. "And do another acid sweep of the unit for the hell of it."

Ingro hurried to his own office and put a call through to Agent Tracy Tips.

"Tips, we've got to head back out to Unit 87 immediately to make an acid sweep."

"What happened? Did Walker find out the C-4 laced bombs we left weren't acid based?"

"The COM just showed activity down there."

"Are you serious?" Agent Tips sounded worried, no doubt realizing if whoever was down there had the brains to look close, it would put a sizeable fork in their collective asses. She and Ingro both knew Walker wouldn't hesitate to kill them both if he got wind of their incompetence.

"Walker thinks it might be story hunters," Ingro said. "Still, he wants us to get out there, get rid of them, and make another sweep. This time, with acid."

"Do we get to kill them?"

"Looks like it."

* * *

Phoenix, Arizona - 11:57 p.m.

Ingro, Tips, and the two Anemen rode in a black, titanium-trimmed, modified UH-10 Iroquois helicopter en route to Unit 87. The mission pilot was Wolf Brigadier, former naval commander and an exiled reconnaissance pilot who first made his name known by discovering nuclear missiles on the shores of Cuba during his first year as a pilot at the age of twenty. At that time, his rank was lieutenant junior grade and his discovery sparked the flame in the Cuban Missile Crisis.

Due to his uncanny reconnaissance abilities, Special Cavalry Services filtered Brigadier into black ops. However, the operations he conducted soon exiled him from the Navy, forcing him to accept any offer made to him.

Brigadier spoke into his headset. "Team, put on your night vision. We're four miles out and closing. I'm shutting off visuals. We're flying blind, people. Agent Ingro, I'm picking up two unknowns, and systems indicate they're heavily armed."

"Story searchers, my ass!" Ingro said to Tips. "Looks like this is more serious than we thought."

"Should I patch a line through to Walker, sir?" Tips asked.

"Are you out of your fucking mind? Let's see exactly what we're dealing with here. Maybe we can stop this shit before anyone's the wiser. Do you read me?"

"Loud and clear, sir."

* * *

Kalista's Compound - 12:00 a.m.

Reggie sat at his console, munching on an apple while monitoring Kalista and Riondro's movements.

"Sis, this healthy food shit is kind of addictive." Reggie leaned back in his chair.

He snapped to attention as lights blinked on the monitor, indicating a helicopter approaching the three-mile perimeter. He tossed the apple aside.

"Heads up, people—you've got company. I suggest you get the hell out!"

Reggie worked vigorously at the console, attempting to identify what Kalista and Riondro were up against.

"This commando shit wasn't on the schedule," he said. "They're closing in fast. Unless you two are ready to turn up the heat, you'd better scram."

"We're on our way out," Riondro said, running through a long tunnel. "How far out are they?"

"About a mile and a half, R.B."

* * *

"Set her down here," Ingro said.

"Setting her down, sir." Brigadier circled the machine and maneuvered toward a clearing.

Ingro addressed the Anemen. "All right, you two head in first. Remember you're up against two heavily armed unknowns down there. We'll be right behind you. COMs activated?"

"Yes, sir!" they said in unison.

"All right, move out. It's imperative we stop these people in their fucking tracks."

Watching the two super-soldiers jog into the darkness, Ingro turned to Brigadier. "Upon any sign of trouble, I want you to get this bitch in the air and move your ass to our position immediately—don't wait for my word. Understood?"

"Affirmative, sir."

"Good. Until then, sit tight." Ingro and Tips moved out.

* * *

Kalista and Riondro climbed through the charred rubble at the chamber's entrance, stepping over a massive amount ripped iron and fiberglass, the sharp debris challenging every footstep. Riondro led the way, his semiautomatic weapon drawn. He arrived at the entrance and signaled the all-clear.

Kalista scanned the perimeter with her night-vision goggles. "Reg, where's the chopper?"

"They landed a mile out. There's four people moving in south of you, so you have a clear shot to the Hummer."

Without hesitation, they both made a run for it, Kalista holding point with Riondro on the flank.

Hearing what sounded like firecrackers, he checked the perimeter to see specks of light flickering in the distance.

"Get down!" he yelled. Finding themselves without cover, they dropped flat to the ground, bullets whizzing over their heads and kicking up dirt around them.

The pair returned fire, both spinning in excess of three clips each, keeping the opposition momentarily at bay.

Reggie patched in from the COM, "I'm sure you're having a ball out there, but I thought you should know, that chopper I mentioned a while ago just left the ground and is headed your way."

"I'll hold them off—get to the Hummer!" Riondro shouted.

"Moving out," Kalista said, returning a few shots before crawling toward the vehicle.

As Riondro covered the area, he was shocked to see a huge man emerge from the tree line and come at him like a charging bull. He fired an entire twenty-five-round clip into the guy, barrel smoking. As the first man crumpled to the ground, a second man came running at Riondro, leaping over his comrade. The man ripped the gun from Riondro's hand and snapped it in half, then landed a fist in his chest, sending him a good fifteen feet through the air.

He hit the ground with the full brunt of his weight, creating a dust cloud that lingered heavily. From the dirt, he took a moment to catch his breath, holding tight to his chest. It felt like he had been hit with a sledgehammer.

Riondro shifted his weight painfully to take a look at the man and was dumbfounded to see he bore no weapon.

"Come on, you son of a bitch," Riondro groaned. He unsheathed the utility knife strapped to his upper shoulder. The Bambokí Iron Horse would do its work if he could only get the man close enough. He heard his headset crackling twenty feet away, Kalista's voice calling for him.

Barreling toward Riondro, the unknown man swung for his face. Just as that fist was about to connect, Riondro lifted his Bambokí with his left hand and supported it with his right, allowing the full force of the guy's punch to land upon the blade. The blade lodged into the man's upper forearm. With a violent twist, Riondro drove the blade down and forcibly split the man's forearm in two.

He jabbed the blade into the man's left shoulder, then pulled it up to the side of the neck, ripping it clean through. He jumped on top of the injured man and buried his blade directly into his heart, twisting the blade left to right. All of it happened before the man could even react.

Riondro hauled himself up. He saw the Hummer activate its lights and immediately veer as, from above, a missile blasted from the dark sky, missing the vehicle by inches. He looked up, barely hearing a low fluttering sound. Suddenly, he was spotlighted by the beam of the helicopter's searchlight. Loading in a clip, he set up to shatter the spotlight, when he was brought to his knees with a throat crunching maneuver.

The arm around his neck felt like an iron bar. Riondro gasped for air before reaching backward for the assailant's testicles and squeezing them with everything he had. The assailant let go, howling. As Riondro turned to face him, he stared in horror at the guy he'd emptied a full clip into. The man's clothing was pocked with bullet holes. On his periphery, Riondro saw the second man get up and brush himself off. In a moment, Riondro knew what he was up against.

"Fuck me," he croaked.

He set off three shots directly into the forehead of the man before him. The assailant fell like a ton of bricks.

Before he could celebrate, the second attacker stripped him of his weapon, snatched him up by the neck, and drew back his fist. Riondro felt his body weaken as oxygen escaped his lungs. He nearly passed out when, from the south, a bullet struck his captor in the back of the head.

"Thank God," Riondro said, spitting out blood. He heard the Hummer churning dirt in the north. He grabbed his gun and began to fire in the direction of the oncoming fire, attempting to get the hell away from these men before they woke up again.

The Hummer drew near, avoiding the entourage of artillery raining down from the chopper. Kalista clipped Riondro's foot as she made a sharp turn to avoid a missile. He made a break for the Hummer, jumped on top of the vehicle and hung on. Kalista fired shots through the roof, narrowly missing him.

"Damn it! Stop shooting, it's me up here!"

"Sorry!"

"You're forgiven if you get us the hell out of here!"

The chopper set off a barrage of missiles toward the Hummer. Squinting his eyes against the whipping wind, Riondro realized the bird was titanium trimmed. The chopper flew low to the ground. With a little luck, he might get a shot off. Riondro reloaded and fired toward the back end, trying to steady his hand despite the moving vehicle under him.

He managed to bend a flank propeller. The blades jammed and smoke spewed from the tail end.

Riondro couldn't help but smile. "I got you, you fuck!"

Moments later, the chopper made a sharp turn, the tail end bursting into flames as it spun out of control.

* * *

Ingro and Tips lowered their weapons, watching the Hummer spin away and disappear in the distance. "Shit," Ingro said. Both Anemen hopped to their feet.

"Did you get a tracer on them?" Ingro asked. "Did you get a good look?"

The one who had been shot in the back of the head was trying to save his clothing in the places where the blood coating his uniform seemed to eat away at the fabric. "I applied tracing dust to his skin, but we have to get back to headquarters ASAP to map out their location."

"And—"

"I didn't get a good look at him. His face was heavily camouflaged, sir."

"All right." Ingro radioed the chopper. "Brigadier, get the fuck down here!"

"It looks like I haven't much choice, sir. I'm hit pretty bad." Brigadier said, then went silent. Moments later, the chopper made a wobbly landing, smoke pouring from the rear end.

Ingro turned to Tips. "Goddammit! Call Walker."

He addressed the Anemen. "You two get down there and set up for the acid sweep immediately."

"Yes, sir." The two men shuffled back toward the wreckage.

* * *

Wincing as he climbed through the Hummer's window, Riondro noticed Reggie's face on the monitor.

"R.B., what happened to you?"

"Those monsters you talked about? They were out there. I'm lucky to be alive."

"You ran into one of them?" Reggie's face lit up.

"Two, actually," Riondro said. "And it was the other way around—they ran into me. I put a full clip into one of them and a few minutes later he got right back up."

"That explains the empty capsules," Kalista said. "Reg, initiate a tracer scan."

"One scan coming up, sis. Wait, I've got something here. R.B., you have tracers on you."

Riondro started patting himself down for bugs, but Reggie laughed. "That's a waste of time. They hit you with dust tracers— it's a new sensory device that came out of Area 51 about two years ago, now used by Special Forces to track the whereabouts of world leaders. Fundamentally, they're nasty little microscopic mechanisms with a mind of their own. When placed on the skin, the little buggers move into your pores and set up shop."

Kalista edged away from Riondro as if he might be contagious.

"Look, R.B., it would be virtually impossible for the average man to deactivate these alien monstrosities, but I, the Wizard, am going to get you all fixed up. Now sit tight."

As Reggie typed, Riondro felt his body tingling slightly, like a feather was tickling him from the inside out.

"You can relax now," Reggie said. "All clean. Your chopper is revved up and ready to go. I'll see you two at home." He winked. "I'm glad you both made it out of that shit alive."

"Oh Reg," Kalista said.

"I'm serious about that. I don't think I could live another day without you fetching my slippers."

"What an asshole!" Kalista was still smiling as she checked her Heckler and Koch P7 M13, making sure it was fully loaded. She placed her weapon on her lap and refocused her attention on the road.

"He's something else, your brother." Riondro said, grabbing an upper side bar as Kalista rolled over a steep gap.

"My brother's been that way for as long as I can remember."

"But he makes you laugh?"

"Yeah, he sure does."

"Well, I guess we'd better get home, and fast."

"Why do you say that?"

"You have to fetch those slippers, remember?" They exchanged smiles.

18

Kalista held an old letter from General Thimpkin. She focused on the poem he'd enclosed.

The forces that are before thee,
I cannot explain, even though
one is experiencing in the physical.
Unseen forces are hard to battle,
for they're strong in this state of being.

May your mind remain strong
for the battle at hand, never
allowing you to fall prey to corruption.
May your strength remain within,
for you are the warrior of your person.

"Hey, sis," Reggie said, pulling up a chair. He sat beside her and put his arm around her shoulders. "You okay, sister soldier? What's this?" He snatched the letter out of her hands playfully. "Are you taking up poetry now? Damn, you're more screwed up than I thought."

"Stinky, don't be stupid." She grabbed the letter back from him and put it inside the digital combination metal case Thimpkin had left for her after the 1998 operation.

Reggie shook his head. "Hey, what's the matter? Are you having flashbacks again?" He peered into her eyes.

She sealed the case and placed it atop her lab counter. "No matter how hard I try, it's still there and I can't seem to shake it. Look, I just want to be alone right now. Do me a favor and check on Riondro for me. I'll be here in the lab for a while."

* * *

A few minutes later Reggie knocked on Riondro's door. He entered to find the man standing in front of the window, his shirt off, gauze dressings were taped over his ribs.

Reggie cuffed him on the shoulder. "Hey, R.B.! What's up, man? Sister soldier told me to check up on you."

"I'm good." Riondro looked up. "Tell me something. What's your story, kid?"

Reggie flopped into a chair, staring around the room. "Kid? I don't see any kid here!"

"So how old are you?"

"Nineteen. I'm getting up there."

Riondro smiled. "What are you doing here? I mean, shouldn't you be in school or something, living it up? You're still a teenager, for God's sake."

"Look around you, R.B. We're in hiding. I could hack myself a new identity to get a GED, but why bother? Don't get me wrong, I can see myself at an Ivy League school, cruising in a high-tech James Bond 1962 Aston Martin DB4. Or maybe a silver 1963 Corvette Sting Ray—you know, the one with the boat-tail rear end and split rear windows?"

"So you like the classic Corvettes?"

"Shit, yeah. Cars, girls, parties—did I mention girls?"

"I think so, Reg."

"I don't like this hiding shit, but it has to be this way at least until all this crap is over with and my sister gets her name back. She's all I have left, and she's gonna shock the world like Rocky Balboa. I mean, what we're working on here is extremely huge. There's no sense going to school if our own government has plans to control the planet."

"Where's your family?"

Reggie raked his hands through his hair. "They're dead. My dad killed my mother, then turned the gun on himself when I was five. Kalista was seventeen."

Riondro walked over and sat on the bed. "I'm sorry," he said quietly.

"Don't be. They fought all the time; my folks gave new meaning to the concept of dysfunction. They were drunks and drug addicts and they took out all their problems on us kids, mostly Kalista. My dad used to do some of the sickest shit to my sister."

Reggie didn't tell Riondro that when he was five, he'd been sleeping in Kalista's bed, trying to comfort her. She lay bruised and naked under the sheets. Hearing their father's drunken footsteps in the hallway, Reggie slid out of bed and scrambled into the closet. Their father, an overweight, dirty man, walked in wearing nothing but a pair of dingy boxer shorts. He slapped Kalista in the face, then climbed on top of her and began raping her. Reggie dug his nails into his hands, shaking with fear and rage.

Snapping out of his reverie, he focused on Riondro sitting beside him.

"I'm sorry," Riondro said. "Nobody should ever have to go through something like that."

Reggie wiped his tears. "Listen, don't tell my sister about this, especially this crying shit. Ever since I was five I've kind of been the man of the house, and you know the man of the house can't show weakness."

"I understand, Reg. After the way you took care of business in the desert, I never want anyone but you watching my back." He knelt beside Reggie. "I'll make you a deal. You keep us safe out there and your secret's safe with me, all right?" Riondro held out his hand for Reggie to shake.

"Cool!" Reggie gave him a high five instead.

"You sure do know your way around computers."

"No prob. Computers are like my family pet. There's nothing I can't do with one. My sister says I'm some kind of a genius. Hell, who am I to argue?"

* * *

Gecko Bravo Compound - June 3, 2003

Walker slammed his sterling Zippo onto the round table.

Seated before him, Doug Ingro, Tracy Tips, Greg Numan, and Debra Hilton winced. The two Anemen looked calm and bored.

"You incompetent fools!" Walker shouted. "Do you have any idea the importance of what we're trying to accomplish here? We can tolerate no interference, because this cannot get out, and if it does, our fucking objective will be shit. I handpicked you fucking idiots to see this through with me—and that was my first mistake. Ingro, it was a stupid move not to acid lace Unit 87 the first fucking time. I should bash your goddamned head in. You, of all people, should know better. Flawless in our methods; flawless in our execution! That's the rule, you fucks. Thank you very much, you fucking idiots, for shitting on this rule."

Walker stood and paced the floor, too angry to sit.

Ingro began, "Yes, sir, but—"

"Shut the fuck up, Agent, before I put a bullet through your thick skull. Whoever those people were, they were damn sure ready for us. We have to get a lead on them ASAP." Walker opened his second pack of cigarettes of the day and lit one. "Whoever they are, we don't know their next move, but they're not to be underestimated, understood? This is not the fucking Boys and Girls Club. We're the fucking National Security Agency, for God's sake. Under no circumstance should our objective be discovered. Get in touch with all your resources and find out who the fuck they are, then wipe them off the face of the planet."

He paused, meeting their eyes one at a time. "People. Flawless in our methods, flawless in our execution. Ingro, you'll lead the team alongside Tips. Right now, I want you all to follow me to the lab."

The group trailed behind Walker down a long, well-lit hallway and stopped in front of a massive iron door. Lifting his hand to a scanner, Walker paused a few seconds until the door slid open, forcing white steam into the hallway. He led the team into a small, well-equipped laboratory that looked down on an empty glass room. The environment resembled the inside hull of a spaceship—white walls, rows of computer equipment, and colorful liquids bubbling on the lab tables. Three scientists wearing full white bodysuits and protective helmets hovered at the entrance like soldiers awaiting orders.

One flight down was a room enclosed in a glass dome, containing four silver tables. The two Anemen and Walker climbed a flight upstairs to the observation booth, where they donned safety gear and helmets.

One of the scientists instructed Ingro, Tips, Numan, and Hilton to step into the glass room. The man closed the door behind them, sealing them inside. Once the door was secure, he gave the observation room the thumbs-up.

Walker's voice echoed over the intercom inside the room. "All of you get naked and lie on the tables."

The team glanced at each other, then at the viewing window. It would be a bad time to disobey an order, no matter how strange.

When they'd removed their clothing and stretched out on the cold steel tables, one of the scientists glanced at Walker, looking for the go-ahead. Walker nodded, and the scientist flipped a series of switches and lifted a small plastic lever to reveal a glowing red button. He pushed the button and within seconds, gray mist filled the room below.

* * *

Kalista's Compound - June 3, 2003

Kalista was seated in front of a lab table, analyzing a specimen, when Riondro entered the room.

Taking her eye away from the lens of her microscope, she glanced over her shoulder. "Did my brother come up there to check on you?"

He sat on the stool beside her. "Yeah, he did. He's a good kid, your brother."

"One of the best."

"So, what did you find out about those samples we brought back?"

She sighed. "It's exactly what I feared. They somehow altered the formula of the original and developed a partially invincible soldier. Something like this would be good in the hands of the right people, but in the hands of the National Security Agency and their friends, it's deadly."

"You said partially invincible?"

"These guys aren't grown in a lab. They started out as real human beings who had their genetic structure altered and enhanced.

And though the genetic enhancement creates internal properties that speed up healing, they can be killed. All we have to do is separate their body parts, giving them no resource for regeneration. That's what happened at the lab in Arizona. Or, we could use a highly potent acid."

She pointed to a table piled with weapons. "I took the liberty of lacing our ammo with extremely potent hydrochloric acid. This stuff will break down the foreign genetics of the serum and cause the soldier's body to deteriorate from inside."

"Sounds like overkill."

She grinned. "The weirdest thing is, some of the DNA strands survive—they seem to lie dormant. I found that these unknown strands of DNA even with intense heat, they can't be killed."

He thought for a moment. "It must be the extraterrestrial DNA from the beings collected at the 1947 crash in Roswell."

"I'm still amazed by this stuff, and the new samples show they've refined it even more. I think the world is in big trouble."

She grabbed two syringes with the serum and set them in front of him.

"We have to become what we're battling," she said.

He leapt to his feet. "You want me to become one of those—those monsters?"

"We'll have a better chance of defeating them before the plan goes fully into effect. If my hunch is correct, their next step will be to find and to eliminate us. We have to move fast to get enough intel to blow this operation wide open, so everyone in our government will know what's going on and recognize the threat to our national security. Exposing them is our best bet."

"This is insane," he said, keeping his distance.

"It's the only way."

"There's got to be—"

"I've patiently waited for you to recover for five years, because I couldn't do this alone. These people have already destroyed so many lives, including your family." She looked deep into his eyes. "Think of how strong you were when you woke from that coma. It was like you'd only been asleep for a night, the way your muscles stayed intact. Think about it! After five years you should have been weak, with no muscle tone. But you would have been no good to me in that condition."

"What are you trying to say?"

With a sigh, she picked up the original capsule of the veteran's blood. "In my research of this first sample, I found and isolated its regenerative characteristics after a year of study and animal testing. I spliced it with a common steroid and injected you quarterly for four years. So, in a sense, your body already contains a piece of the extraterrestrial DNA in your bloodstream."

"You—"

"Do you remember the explosion? Do you remember February 26, 1993?"

He flashed back to the day he watched his family walk into the World Trade Center building.

She continued, watching him closely. "I found hidden locations they used to test and develop this serum. Every time they came closer to their objective, they did a total wash of anyone who might know about the project outside their department. Your family was caught in the crossfire."

He leaned against the table, hands over his face. She put her arms around him.

"I remember," he said. "I remember, I remember. They killed my wife—my two little boys." Tears streamed down his face. After a few moments, he removed his hands from his face and stared at Kalista, the only person who could comfort him. In her eyes, he saw that compassion and love.

Slowly, their faces moved closer. Just before their lips touched, Reggie strolled into the lab, reading a magazine.

"You guys have to see this shit, they—"

Reggie looked up, then quickly spun around and headed for the door.

Riondro blinked, then felt his face turn red. "I guess we should get started," he said.

* * *

Kalista's Compound - June 24, 2003

Three weeks later, Kalista and Riondro worked together in the lab, prepping themselves for the unpredictable scientific procedure. She had delayed things so she could test the serum again, hoping to be absolutely sure of their safety. In her years of research and study, she'd never had the means or opportunity to test the serum on a human subject. All her theories had been based on animal tests.

In spite of the outward confidence she displayed in her convincing Riondro to undergo the procedure with her, she still had doubts. But they had to go forward with her plan—there was no other choice and she would do or say anything to achieve her objective.

Once he agreed to the procedure, she'd thoroughly studied their blood, metabolism, and anatomy. She put both of them through a detailed work-up before giving the green light to continue.

Wearing skintight protective uniforms, the two soldiers lay on medical tables in the lab as Reggie stood in front of them, prepared to inject the serum.

"Here goes nothing." Reggie said, placing his thumb on the syringe. "Sis, you're sure about this?"

"It's okay." She placed a reassuring hand on his arm.

"All right." Reggie injected first Riondro, then Kalista with the serum.

Fifteen minutes later, they both developed a queasy feeling, followed by an hour of nausea. Then, they were suddenly hit hard with an overwhelming sensation of feverish anxiety blended with excruciating pain. The sensation stretched for an unbelievable forty-five minutes and fifty-two seconds as they squirmed on the tables in agony. They endured the pain stoically. After what seemed a lifetime, the worst of it passed and the painful muscle cramps eased, followed by a sublime sensation that rolled over them both as if they were tipsy.

"You two sit tight," Reggie said. "The worst is over. I'll be back in an hour or so to check up on you. If you need me, just whistle."

"So how long does this take?" Riondro turned to look at Kalista, stretched on a table beside him.

She stared at the ceiling. "By my calculations, it should take no more than five hours. I concentrated the serum and recalculated so it would target specific organs at once."

"What's next after this?"

"We get our names back and quite possibly save the world. How does that sound?"

He laughed. "Save the world! Sounds like something out of a comic book, huh?"

"Yeah."

"Tell me something. Has anyone ever told you how beautiful you are?"

She grinned. "I never gave anybody a chance to get that close."

He returned a serious look. "I know about what happened to you. I know about your family."

"How?"

"Reggie told me."

"Damn Reggie." She closed her eyes.

"Hey, I asked."

"I know."

"He's losing out on being a kid, you know."

"Look, I've been taking care of my brother all his fucking life, so don't tell me what I'm not doing for him."

"Sure, but—"

"I didn't ask for this! I was assigned to a routine mission, which turned out to be a fucking national conspiracy."

"Sorry. I didn't mean anything."

She looked around the room. "Did you ever wonder how I could afford all this stuff? Thimpkin gave this stuff to me."

"General George Thimpkin? As in, the most decorated general in the United States Armed Forces?"

"I served in his company. He and I had, like, a special relationship."

"I had no idea. You two—"

"Not *that* kind of relationship." She sighed. "He was like a father to me. A good father, I mean. Don't get me wrong, he didn't take it easy on me. In fact, he was harder on me because he could see right through me. He knew my demons."

"So he became your father?"

She looked up at the ceiling. "On the day of our mission into Vietnam, Thimpkin was the one who saved our lives. We didn't have any other way out of there."

Another memory rolled through Riondro's mind; this one hazy, swimming in unconsciousness. "He was there that day," he said.

"You were unconscious."

"No, I remember. He came roaring through the sky like a gray ghost."

"I watched a rocket launcher fire the shell that destroyed his chopper." She was quiet for a moment. "He died that day saving our lives."

"I didn't know."

"What's more, he'd already planned for me to disappear after that mission, because he knew what these creeps were up to. This facility we're in was an old underground communications warehouse of his that I altered to be what you see here. Plus five million in cash and untraceable bonds."

"He was your guardian angel," Riondro said. *Just like you are to me*, he thought.

* * *

Reggie walked into the lab, "Okay, sweethearts—let's see if this serum really packs a punch."

He helped them both to an upright position on the lab tables. For the next hour, the pair went through a series of tests they'd planned in advance. They passed every obstacle, proving beyond any doubt that the serum was magnificent.

This was a work of sheer genius!

Now she knew why the unknowns behind this project allowed nothing and no one to stand in their way. She also knew that to produce and cover up an operation of this magnitude, the people involved had to be cold, heartless, and utterly maniacal. She knew this serum was far beyond anything mankind had even contemplated.

Their final hurdle was hand-to-hand combat. Reggie looked on, amazed at what he witnessed as they sparred.

"You ready?" she asked.

"Shit, yeah."

"Ready for what, you guys?" Reggie spoke over the speaker that echoed inside the gym.

Kalista and Riondro suddenly charged each other. He punctured her arm straight through to the bone. Blood splattered onto the floor and she landed hard against the wall.

Reggie charged into the room. "Sis!"

"Reg—look!" Riondro stared at Kalista's arm.

The wound was already healing itself; the shattered bone mended, then the veins, muscles, and connective tissue. Finally, the wound sealed itself with no trace of a scar.

They were momentarily quiet, looking at each other in amazement. Then the three burst into laughter.

"We're ready for whatever they throw at us." Kalista said.

An alarm sounded behind them from Reggie's console. "I'll leave you two to lick your wounds," he said, heading upstairs.

On the monitors, he saw Nurse Hanna standing outside their front door, trying to peer in the window.

"What in the hell is she doing here?" he said. "Sis!"

Kalista took one look and picked up a weapon from a side table. "I'm going up there. Keep an eye on her."

"You don't think—"

"We can't take any chances."

Riondro walked in as Kalista ran out.

"Your nurse is back," Reggie said.

"Is she trying to get her job back?"

Reggie laughed. "She just wants to give you another sponge bath."

Riondro leaned in. "She looks nervous."

* * *

Kalista hurried through the kitchen and approached the front door. She leaned on the side of the door, gun raised. "Who is it?"

At first, she got no response. She listened to a shuffling sound outside.

"It's me. Hanna."

Kalista waited for the wisecrack, but Hanna didn't launch into their usual playful routine.

"Yeah," Kalista prompted. "Prove it!"

Outside, Hanna began to cry. "Please, just let me in. Please."

"Hanna, what's the matter with you?"

"Just let me in, please. Hurry."

Kalista unlocked the door to find Hanna in tears. As she grabbed the woman's coat and pulled her inside, Reggie's voice came over the intercom.

"Sis, we've got trouble—I'm seeing six black vans around the house. Hold on, I'm picking up something else. I can't seem to get a clear readout—it's causing some kind of distortion to my system I've never seen before. I think your nurse is wired with some kind of device—"

Kalista forced the jacket open and discovered a bomb wired to the woman's chest, shielded with some sort of reinforced guard.

"They made me do it—" Hanna sobbed.

"Sis, get your ass out of there." Reggie's voice held a note of panic. "You have less than ten seconds!"

"I'm sorry!" Kalista said to the old nurse before darting toward the corridor.

Hanna screamed, and within seconds the explosives detonated, ripping her body into shreds of bloody flesh and shards of bone. Flames riding her back, Kalista dashed into the secret corridor and once inside, flipped a switch that sealed it airtight. The fire outside the corridor's entrance triggered an extinguishing mechanism that doused the area as Kalista ran back to the underground sanctuary.

* * *

From their van, Ingro and Tips watched the explosion rock the front end of the house, a blast so powerful it momentarily blinded them both. After the blast, Doug Ingro radioed his team.

"Okay, everybody move in. Do a quick sweep and make sure you discover three bodies—I repeat, three fucking bodies."

The sweeper team left their vans and quickly went to work in the front yard, putting out the flames and searching for the bodies.

* * *

Kalista walked into the communications room, brushing debris from her clothing, her face blackened with soot. Pushing Riondro out of the way, she headed straight for Reggie's console.

"Is the house completely destroyed?"

Her brother gulped. "Oh, yeah, it's toast. How the fuck did they find us?"

"Is there any way we can get a camera up there to see what's going on?" Riondro asked.

"No problemo. I've got a few ground level cameras around the compound just for this occasion. Here we go—"

Over the monitor, they watched a team dressed in black combat gear performing a sweep of the rubble. Reggie scanned in and got a shot of the men and women, all in suits, overlooking the sweep.

"Wait a minute." Riondro moved closer. "I recognize that face."

At the World Trade Center, he'd gotten a good look at Doug Ingro's face among men and women in black hurrying out back. He would have forgotten, but Agent Ingro had removed his glasses, revealing his silver eye patch.

Riondro checked his AK-47, saw it was fully loaded, and advanced toward the door.

Kalista grabbed him and turned him around to face her. He shoved her aside, but she followed, spun him around, and knocked the AK out of his hands. She maneuvered him to his knees as he struggled to break free.

"Riondro, goddammit! We're going to finish this, but right now is not the time. We can't afford to give up our location, and we can't afford for them to know we're alive!"

"Surely they'll realize we're alive soon," he said. "We've got to go do something."

Reggie grinned from his position at the monitor. "Get a load of this, R.B. Years ago, we stashed two sets of skeletal remains under the floorboards. By the looks of it, their sweeper team just found the package and took the bait."

Kalista grabbed Reggie's shoulder. "We'll hit the Gecko Bravo Branch tonight. You'll be guiding us through, so get out those old maps of yours and get to work. We'll head out at nightfall. Now that they think we're dead, we've got ultimate freedom."

"And then I'll get that bastard," Riondro said. "Now if you'll excuse me, I've got to put in a little range practice."

Kalista clapped her brother on the back. "If I can make it through this, we'll be free to do all the things we've been putting off. Think about it—I can finally travel around the world as a civilian, you can go back to high school and be a regular kid."

"You mean, I can go on dates and everything?"

"I don't know if you're smooth enough with the ladies, Reg."

"Quit playing!"

"Seriously, though." Kalista held her brother's shoulders tight. "This could be it."

19

Ingro, Tips, Numan, Hilton, and the two Anemen reported to Walker's office. Walker stood at his window, gazing into the distance while playing with his silver Zippo. The team quietly took seats at the round table.

"Do you chucklefucks have news for me?" Walker asked.

"Sir, our hunch was right in deciding to initiate a thorough background check on conspiracy theorists," Ingro said. "We logged more than six thousand names, but two stood out: living in seclusion outside New York, with zero history prior to 1998. Their names were George Watson and Trina Oskins. No bank accounts, no paper trail. They built the whole place just five years ago financed in cash."

"Rich kids."

"More like rich kids who appeared one day from nowhere. No neighbors within ten miles of their residence, no friends. They didn't pay for water service, electricity, nothing."

"So they're rich ghosts."

"Right. Then, we checked further. We learned that General Thimpkin once owned the land, under the name of his late father—

one four-star General Henry C. Thimpkin. This land has been in the Thimpkin family for generations."

The tapping of Walker's Zippo grew almost imperceptibly louder when Ingro mentioned General Thimpkin.

"The thing that got us was, General Thimpkin signed over the land—land that had been in his family for generations—to this Trina Oskins."

"Wasn't that generous of him."

"We think something else was going on."

"Obviously, numbnuts."

Ingro grimaced. "We found a nurse who told us she was there taking care of a coma victim inside the house for five years. She also gave us the gem that her patient miraculously recovered, so she no longer worked at the residence."

"A ready-made mole."

"Exactly, sir. We sent her back and got a shot of Trina Oskins." Ingro signaled for Agent Tips to pass the series of photos they'd taken at the doorway.

"It's Kalista Flaker," Walker said, glancing at the photo before tossing it away. "Goddammit, it's her. Thimpkin knew enough about our objective to bury us all along."

"But, sir," Ingro said, "We eliminated them and destroyed the place. There should be no problems."

"Oh, no problems, fantastic." Walker said. "Did you find the fucking bodies?"

"Yes, sir, we found the remains of two bodies, plus the scattered remains of the nurse."

"Did you even attempt to analyze the remains for a DNA match with Flaker and Thimpkin?"

"Sir, when we took our samples of the two bodies, the DNA work-up showed the remains belonged to Captain Flaker and her brother Reginald Milwaukee Flaker." Ingro passed the paper to his boss, who waved it off. "After that, we then concluded our discovery and evidence sweep. Sir, no one could have made it out of that house alive. The explosive used was the classified C8-476-12-Z Cobra Flash Stinger."

"Wasn't that the same weapon used in 1993, at the World Trade Center?"

Ingro nodded. "It never fails, sir."

Walker sat down heavily. "We can't push on until we have complete confirmation that there's no further interference with our objective. We don't even know if the information they obtained has been leaked to anyone."

Agent Tips spoke up. "Sir, even if they did have information, I don't think they had any physical proof. Nothing to warrant an internal investigation."

"Captain Flaker could get herself out of hell with a glass of ice water. I want all of you on red alert. Use as many agents as possible to secure this branch. If they're still alive, their next stop will be here to get the physical proof they need to expose the project. That cannot happen, people!"

Tips leaned forward. "With all due respect, sir, who could they tell? We're all aware that Project Aneman was created by an anonymous collective—we don't even know who they are. All we know is this is a massive conspiracy and we're just the foot soldiers."

Walker gave her a thin smile. "Your candor is commendable, Tips. Are you questioning my authority?"

Ingro pulled his side arm and placed it on the table directly in front of Walker.

Tips adjusted herself in her chair. "I didn't mean any disrespect, sir."

After a long pause, Walker glanced at Ingro, who reclaimed his weapon.

"Yes, this is bigger than all of us," Walker said. "Exposing this project would tear this country apart, diminishing our standing as a superpower and world leader. If these rogue agents succeed, they'll destroy the work we've been doing since 1947."

"The work?" Tips asked.

"I know this was before you were born, but listen up. In 1947 our organization activated phase two of Project Aneman after an unbelievable discovery in Roswell, New Mexico—extraterrestrial life and technology. During the study of these beings and their metabolism, geneticists isolated an unusual strand of DNA that proved to have miraculous properties. With these properties, our scientists strongly felt we could eventually create what every military in the world wants: a super soldier.

"As Sun Tzu states in The Art of War, 'All warfare is based on the art of deception.' Project Aneman was developed with this philosophy in mind. Though it took more time than we expected to reach this point in the project, this operation was forged primarily to seal America's superpower status long before the turn of the twentieth century. Vietnam was the only war in which the beta version of the serum was tested. In November 1962, because Kennedy was considering withdrawing our troops from Vietnam, we negotiated with Johnson, giving him fundamental information about Project Aneman and our plans. It wasn't too difficult to bring him aboard—he had a beef of his own with Kennedy. He felt the man's liberal politics were ruining the country, taking us backwards. Like many others, Johnson thought this Irish goody-goody, Ivy League, wet-behind-the-ears kid wasn't worth the shoes he was wearing."

Tips raised her hand to ask a question, but Walker ignored her.

"Project Aneman happened to be the perfect sharpened sword to cut the head off that fucking Oval Office gigolo. Johnson wanted the presidency, and he'd have done damn near anything to get it. We, on the other hand, didn't give a good goddamn about Johnson's motivations. He was just our puppet. We wanted to test our serum on a massive level, and we knew he would honor his part in the agreement, pushing forward the assault on Vietnam. Johnson hoped to strengthen his political ties and his legacy with an unquestionable victory in Vietnam, and we expected much more out of the serum."

Walker lit another cigarette and tossed the empty pack away. "Unfortunately, our test failed. We ended up killing more Americans than we planned—our scientists had developed some new form of bottled insanity that slowly overcame every one of the American soldiers we injected in the field. This serum created psychopathic madmen, most incapable of combat, making them prime targets for capture.

"Of course, we wrote those casualties off, as we always do, as collateral damage. Johnson was responsible to clean it all up. Hell, this asshole consciously made a deal with the devil, so what did he expect?" At this, Walker laughed—a high-pitched, humorless sound.

"This new form of bottled insanity was known as J-XXX-0602, or JAXX. It was far from what we expected, but proved useful in many operations after the fact—one being Ronald Reagan and his would-be assassin, John W. Hinckley Jr. Our objective in that scenario was to upgrade yet another vice president—this time, George H.W. Bush, Senior. Instead of an assassination, which would put too much heat on Bush, our objective was to drive Reagan mad. Using the JAXX serum, we meant to drive him insane to the point where the nation would clearly see their president was off his fucking rocker. After witnessing this, we hoped America would accept Vice President Bush as their president, despite his questionable background.

"So we injected JAXX into John W. Hinckley's system and over time got him to believe Ronald Reagan was literally the antichrist." Walker smugly laughed under his breath. "Just for kicks, I convinced Hinckley that Jodi Foster was in love with him.

The shot was actually made by our black ops agents—Hinckley's dumb ass couldn't shoot a bowling ball off a stick if it was five feet in front of him—and the bullet that hit President Reagan in the chest was laced with a small amount of JAXX. Black ops fled the scene, leaving Hinckley behind to take the fall. He had a field day shooting around like a madman! The dose of the serum we laced the bullet with did take effect, but it proved too weak to completely overcome Reagan during his presidency. However, that serum definitely worked some wicked magic on his body and mind."

Walker grinned. "Hinckley's part in our ongoing affairs is still useful to us. Ladies and gentlemen, since February '99 we've had an ongoing mission in play. We injected Hinckley with the experimental 10-558-GI serum, which stabilized his mental state so we could get him released from the mental institution on unsupervised family visits. We still need Hinckley for another mission of extreme importance. He'll be used to stop one of the two likely 2008 Democratic presidential candidates—Hilary Rodham Clinton or Barack Hussein Obama." He winked at Debra Hilton, who blushed. "Of course, I'm not at liberty to discuss the details of that mission, but from what I've told you, I'm sure you can imagine the rest."

Walker took a drag of his cigarette, looking out the window. "It's the year 2003 and we're again at war. Iraqi Freedom could benefit greatly from Aneman even at this stage, but as we all know, there's a problem hovering over our fucking heads, thanks to our failure to eliminate Thimpkin, Flaker, and God knows who the fuck else back in '98. Oh, and let us not forget our failure at properly sweeping Unit 87 the first goddamn time." He threw a pointed look at Ingro, who looked away.

Walker sighed. "Still," he said, "we continue to push on in our objective to create an unstoppable world superpower and a new world order. We're already causing chaos in Iraq, killing our own comrades to make a fucking point. We're currently staging operations around the world, primarily acting as cloaked instigators in order to push this terrorism propaganda forward.

"Our overall objective will be threatened if the Democratic Party gains the presidential seat. We're already on the verge of cutting the head off the dragon in Iraq, and then we'll focus on Saudi Arabia—another world leader in oil production. If these two nations are conquered, countries of the world will have no choice but to turn to the United States for oil. Tips!"

Agent Tips startled in her seat. "Yes, sir?"

"Are you aware of the Halliburton Corporation?"

She squinted her eyes. "Dick Cheney's company?"

Walker laughed. "Exactly. But much more. Halliburton's part in the overall objective has been grossly misunderstood by the average American. Once the United States gains the power and authority, we will then, with the assistance of Halliburton, occupy and drill for oil in the region of the Caspian Sea. You see, the Caspian Sea region has the world's largest oil reserves, an amazing six trillion dollars' worth, making the Middle East look like a carnival sideshow. The problem has long been our ability to pipe it out. Afghanistan occupies a strategic position between the Caspian Sea and the markets of the Indian subcontinent and East Asia. It's prime territory for building pipelines, which is why the oil company Unocal, as well as the United States government, welcomed the Taliban's rise to power in 1996, as a promising source of stability. Although this stability didn't materialize, people like George W. Bush and the powerful oilmen around him have never given up on the tremendous profit possibilities Central Asia offers. We cannot allow Asia or anyone else to gain control of that resource. The United States' ultimate goal is to build a massive pipeline, carrying the Caspian Sea oil across Afghanistan and down through Pakistan to ports on the Arabian Sea. Along with our occupation of Iraq and Saudi Arabia, gaining control of Caspian Sea oil will make us truly the world's greatest power—and, with that, the world's greatest enemy. And so we must be prepared to defend ourselves, for at all times we'll be looking over our shoulders, keeping a watchful eye out for resistance.

"A force as powerful as the Aneman will be of great importance to the United States in order to protect our new assets. It's always been about the oil! If you control the world's oil markets, you control the world. Project Aneman will be nothing but the icing on the cake after that—icing that will undoubtedly shock the world when it's administered, for America will no longer need these puny nations we call our allies.

"After our success, once a perfect serum is developed, a genetically enhanced military will make a massive strike on the world, occupying territory without fear. For the past twenty years, we've eliminated countless prominent scientists in order to seal the developmental process of Project Aneman from getting away from us.

"People, at this time we're still in the political stages of our objective. If our plans go off without a hitch, President George W. Bush will continue his presidency into 2008. This is absolutely essential for the objective and there's nothing we won't do to accomplish his re-election. We put him there in the first place, so he owes it to us."

Walker continued, his eyes slightly wild with power. "Did you know that the 1993 attack on the World Trade Center was dual-pronged? It served as an attempt to create anarchy within the Clinton administration and also destroy one of our testing labs and the scientists. And, of course, to draw world attention to terrorism and publicize those fucking Islamic extremists.

"Then, ladies and gentlemen, came September 11. In my opinion, the final attack on the World Trade Center towers was a work of art—Picasso couldn't touch it. The planning took place months into the Gore-Bush presidential race, simultaneously with our plan to tamper with the vote. In New York, black ops agents posed as window cleaners and placed explosive foundation tumblers into the walls of both buildings, rigged so they could be detonated from a distance. When the planes struck the towers, we left plenty of time for the media to take their pictures, then record and transmit live footage to the world. After enough time had passed and the world was eating this terrorism shit up, we detonated the tumblers and brought those foreign bitches to their fucking knees. We made a monstrous statement by killing more than three thousand American citizens to further our cause. The funny thing about it all was that, in watching the footage of the towers coming down, how could people not see something strange? Those two towers were massively fortified. It would have been virtually impossible to completely bring them down that way, especially with only one plane per tower. But America and the world ate that shit up like dinner."

Walker stubbed his cigarette out and lit another. "You know something? Americans never cease to amaze me with their stupidity. They'd believe I had Bigfoot suck my dick last night if I told them my story with a clearance badge on."

The agents laughed.

"September 11 forced Congress to get off their fucking asses and back our president, which in turn fed directly into the objective. We finally had detailed intelligence of Saddam Hussein's whereabouts just weeks into the media hype circling Operation Iraqi Freedom. We captured him and brought him here for torture—I mean, questioning. On November 27, President Bush is scheduled to leave the United States under a shroud of secrecy to Iraq to visit with our troops—supposedly for Thanksgiving. A drugged Hussein will actually be Air Force One's cargo. The objective is to place Hussein in a 'spider hole' in his hometown of Tikrit. The hole is scheduled to be dug on September 16 by Black Ops field agents. Hussein will be taken into custody by an American ground force on December 13. An early Christmas present! He was actually a prisoner of the United States from the very day we began the assault on Iraq.

"Project Aneman is a venture more important than half of you in this room will ever know. In wartime, America would have no problem establishing her dominance over the world, made possible by our massive band of unstoppable Anemen. No force on God's green earth could stand up to America's fierce campaign to occupy world territory. In time, America will control this planet, creating the long-awaited new world order. All warfare is based on the art of deception, and we no longer have the benefit of deception. If Project Aneman is exposed, the upper hand will be lost."

Walker returned to his chair with a self-satisfied grin. "Now that you know this project has so many tentacles, Agent Tips, I hope you understand that questioning the process or speculating about it will only bury you."

Tips nodded. "I understand, sir."

He paused, looking contemplatively at the photo of Kalista pulling Hanna inside the compound. "We've had a noose around our necks since you and I came aboard this project," he said. "The only way out is through death."

Walker studied the photograph before him. "Your mistakes ultimately become my mistakes," he said, leaning close as if talking to the picture. "Karma is one barbaric, hellish bitch I'd rather keep away from, because I know with my deeds, past and present, I'll have hell to pay." He looked up. "Am I understood?"

"Yes, sir!" the agents respond in unison.

Walker slammed his hand on the tabletop. "Secure the fucking facility—now!"

After everyone left his office, Walker dialed the lab.

"This is Walker. Did you prepare the facility?"

"Yes, sir. We're awaiting your arrival."

"And the modifications?"

"Yes sir, the modifications we created for you will quicken the effect ratio."

"Fine. I'm on my way." Walker hung up the phone and grabbed a pack of cigarettes from his desk on his way out of his office.

* * *

Gecko Bravo Compound - June 24, 2003

At 6:15 p.m. the sun was setting below the hills, leaving an orange afterglow reflecting from the clouds. As the sun disappeared over the horizon, it folded a dusty shadow over the well-guarded Gecko Bravo compound.

For the last two hours, Kalista and Riondro had watched the sunset from a secure location high in the hills overlooking the Gecko Bravo compound. The area was sporadically hot with area security, but the pair were more interested in the natural spectacle.

"Absolutely beautiful!" she said, staring at the sun's afterglow.

"Makes you want to never leave."

She checked her watch. "Reggie's due to report in fifteen minutes. We'd better get ready."

"All right."

A distant noise cut their reverie. "Oh, shit," she said, "get down—choppers!"

They dropped to the ground, hiding in the rocky curves of the hillside. The helicopters hovered near their location for several minutes, causing them both to ready their guns. After a few tense minutes, the birds were gone as quick as they came.

Riondro popped up moments later. Rising to her feet as well, Kalista shook her head. "That was close." Before moving closer to the facility, they had watched the guarded perimeter around the Gecko Bravo Branch expand tremendously. From a distance they'd scanned the facility with digitally enhanced binoculars, studying the best way inside.

With her knowledge of guerrilla tactics and special level compound guardianship, Kalista felt it was necessary to get their asses out there and plant themselves in a secure location near the compound before nightfall. From base, her brother agreed with this idea, because he wanted his sensors placed in close proximity to the compound where he could pick up on pertinent details that his system overlooked.

Reggie came in over their headsets. "Are we ready to rock and roll?"

"Yeah, Reg, we're ready," Riondro responded.

"Okay, then, get to your designated point immediately— you're cleared, but you'd better move fast; you only have a seven-minute window. Go, go, go!"

The pair took off across the rocky terrain. Quickly reaching point, they positioned themselves between a series of large carrier trucks that sat parked in a lot. Riondro noticed the facility was more alive than it had been during the two hours they'd evaluated the grounds.

Reggie came back on. "Damn, you two ran two miles in three and a half minutes. That was a record even for you. How does it look at ground level?"

"Looks like a full perimeter lockout," Riondro said. "They're definitely expecting a breach of some sort."

"What's next, little brother?"

"About seventeen meters to the left you'll find a manhole. Be extra careful, because the facility walls are reinforced with some sort of unknown alloy. It's nothing we can't handle, but I'm also showing our verbal communications will be distorted while you're in there."

"Any good news?"

"I just made an excellent ham sandwich?"

Kalista snorted. "Reg, stop fucking around."

"All right, all right. The real good news is that I'll get communication from you, and you'll still be able to see what's going on from my monitor."

"Flying deaf but not blind," Kalista said. "Let's move."

They made it to the manhole within seconds. A pair of guards crossed paths before it, but a low retaining wall provided just enough cover.

Riondro evaluated the manhole. "Reg, are you dropping off at this point?"

"Once you get past the sewage lines, I'll be able to communicate with you again. This alloy seems to be segregated in parts of the sewage areas only."

"Guess that's going to have to be good enough."

"Remember, once you get down there you'll be entirely on your own, so listen up. Go straight down until you reach an old caged opening. You'll have to burn your way through with the welding torch. It's damn near medieval, so it may take quite a while to cut through. That's about forty feet from your entrance. Once you breach the opening, you'll travel exactly three miles until you reach a giant filtration system that cuts across your path and continues for about a hundred yards. You'll have to find your way across in order to continue toward your point, which you'll reach after traveling another two miles. At the end of your two-mile hike, you'll find a ventilation shaft. I want you to position yourselves in the shaft and wait for a call from me. By that time, you'll have made it to the heart of the facility. Once you get to this point, we'll have mutual communication. You got that?"

"Got it!" the pair responded in unison.

"We're out!" Riondro spun his gun around to his back and readied himself to lift the manhole cover.

"Hey, R.B.?"

"Yeah, Reg, what is it?"

"Take care of my sister for me, big man."

Riondro smiled. "That's affirmative—I'm out."

Kalista and Riondro lifted the heavy iron manhole cover, sliding it out of the way so they both could enter. The putrid smell engulfed them both as they worked. A normal human couldn't have lifted it, but their new abilities made it a relatively simple task. Looking inside, they saw a narrow eighty-foot drop that ended in a stream of sewage. An old iron ladder was welded to the wall of the upright tunnel. Riondro climbed down first. He waited below while she slid the cover back in place.

"You feel that?" Riondro asked quietly. His blood was pumping hard and he felt strangely euphoric.

"Yeah, I do."

"What do you think it is?"

Kalista looked around. "It seems like every time we use our abilities, they get stronger. I felt it when we set off toward our initial point."

"I did, too." Riondro spoke into his communicator. "Reg, I know we can't hear you, but I assume you can hear us. I want you to do a scan and check us out thoroughly—we need to know if anything's happening to us. We think something's going on. Out!"

* * *

When they reached the gate, Riondro produced a mini-welding torch, put on a set of goggles, and began burning his way through the heavily reinforced metal. Meanwhile, Kalista watched and listened. Since it was taking a while for him to torch his way through the cage, she decided to check the area further.

She signaled to him. "I'm going further down to check the perimeter." She spoke softly, patting him on the back.

He gave a nod. "All right. Be careful."

Connecting and assembling a utility rope, she inverted herself and slid down the vertical tunnel. The total distance from the position of the cage where Riondro was hard at work burning his way through to the main sewage line was exactly fifty-three feet. As she moved deeper down the line, she soon reached the flowing sewage and saw a conglomeration of tunnels. The place was massive.

She hung there silently inverted for a while, readying her guns when she heard a noise behind her. Twisting around to look, she saw a swarm of rats, a hundred at least, moving in her direction. She quickly signaled Riondro to cut the flame as she angled her way back up through the canal, pinning herself against the wall.

They waited. After the rats was silence, and after the silence was footsteps. Two men dressed in black combat gear and armed with flashlights moved slowly past their position. After they passed, she moved further down the sewage line, watching the men walk into one of the connecting tunnels.

She signaled the all-clear to Riondro and he continued his attempts at breaching the caged opening.

* * *

On Reggie's monitor, two white dots indicated Kalista and Riondro; another two dots represented the scouts. Reggie watched the scouts move steadily away from Kalista and Riondro's position, then suddenly stop. "What's going on here?"

The two dots held still for a minute, then began moving back toward Kalista and Riondro's location. "Guys, get the fuck out of there!" Reggie shouted, knowing they couldn't possibly hear him.

* * *

Riondro finished burning through the caged opening and signaled Kalista to move out. She started back toward his position, climbing the rope she'd assembled. Upon arriving, she disconnected her grappling hook and was the first to climb into the newly opened corridor, entering a six-foot-tall iron shaft.

"They're back," he whispered urgently.

Extending a small mirror outward, he saw the same two men standing quietly in the flow of sewage water at the end of the shaft. The men listened for several seconds then peered upward and into the tunnel in their direction—shining their flashlights toward the open corridor. Pulling back the viewing mirror, he leaned out of the corridor and set off four shots, two into the head of each man.

The scouts fell into the filthy water and he watched them for a minute to see if they were like the monstrous men he had encountered in the Arizona desert. Seeing no movement, he quickly entered the corridor.

"You got 'em?" Kalista asked.

"What do you think?" Riondro smiled.

* * *

Walker and Ingro peered over the team of operators' shoulders, assessing the grounds around the compound on a massive display of monitors.

"What have we got?" Walker asked the line of operators.

"Sir, our Anemen Agents are combing the sewage line, but they haven't reported back yet, sir."

"Ingro, seal this facility tight—every possible access. Radio the guards to close the gates and move inside."

"Yes, sir." In the corridor, Ingro received a call from one of the Anemen.

"Sir, we witnessed one person enter through the upper sewage corridor. It looks like he got into the facility through the eastern manhole."

"You were late in reporting, Agent."

"Sir, upon discovery, we were hit."

Ingro drove his fist against the wall. "Go after him and eliminate him. I want no mistakes. Are we clear?"

"Yes, sir."

Ingro immediately patched a line through to the other agents at Gecko Bravo. "We have a breach. Move your teams in for a full facility shutdown ASAP."

* * *

After traveling a good three miles, Kalista and Riondro finally reached the filtration system Reggie had described. Before them stood a massive dome at least a hundred yards straight across and six hundred feet straight down. A series of iron pipes crisscrossed forty feet above them.

The area was designed with miles of tubing, insulation, and fireproof foam along the walls. The dome was also lined through and through with reinforced positioning wires. Just as Reggie predicted, the filtration system placed a hundred yards of distance between where they stood and where they needed to be in order to carry on with the operation. Their objective was directly in front of them—but clear on the other side of the dome, with no accessible way across. If they failed, the drop was about six hundred feet.

The pair hooked safety guards to their belts, tossing a line around of the sturdy pipes above.

A series of shots suddenly ricocheted down the tunnel, whizzing past their heads. Readying their weapons, they turned and returned fire.

"Are you hit?" Riondro asked, seeing Kalista shudder.

"The bastards got me in the leg!"

"Get your ass across and take cover."

She shimmied up her harness as fast as she could, wedging herself between the pipes that stood forty feet above. The gunshot wound burned, but she felt her leg healing. She double-timed to the other side, returning fire without quite seeing her assailant, positioning herself in a secure area.

Meanwhile, Riondro braved the bullets whizzing by and swung himself back toward their starting point. He climbed back just in time to witness two men firing in their direction. He then saw one of the men indicate to the other that they would change position. Riondro waited in the shadow.

Footsteps grew louder and one of the men passed directly in front of him. When he was close enough, Riondro reached out, snatched away his gun, and broke it in half. He punched the man in the chest, shoving him against the pipes.

They met in hand-to-hand combat. Riondro bent back the man's right knee, ripping the fibers in his leg and breaking the kneecap. When the man gasped with pain, Riondro shoved a pearl of hydrochloric acid into his mouth and shattered the capsule between the agent's teeth by slamming the man's mouth shut with a well-placed kick to the jaw.

"Turnabout is fair play, you fuck." Riondro smiled, knowing the man was dead this time.

Meanwhile, Kalista was heavily engaged in a gunfight with the other assailant.

Riondro positioned himself near the action and radioed to her: "Cease fire. I have this bastard."

He crept up silently behind the man and tapped him on the shoulder. When the man spun around, Riondro sliced his Adam's apple with his ready knife. While the creep dropped to his knees, Riondro readied a shoulder-fire rocket launcher and stood back with a smile on his face.

"Later, asshole."

The fiery shell struck the man in the chest. He exploded in midair and pieces of him rained down six hundred feet.

Kalista popped her head up from the other end of the chasm. She grinned at her mission partner. "If you're done playing, can we finish this mission?"

He shrugged. "If you insist."

* * *

"Aneman Team—report! Do you copy?"

Walker observed Ingro's frantic radio call. "What's the problem, Agent?"

"Sir, our Anemen agents are delayed in reporting again."

"What was their delay the first time?" Walker asked, setting his jaw.

"They were hit by gunfire from one intruder."

"Is the compound fully sealed?"

"All teams have reported and are on their way in to rendezvous with me in your office."

Walker turned away, then paused. "Forget about sending anyone after the Anemen. They're dead."

* * *

By following Reggie's detailed instructions, Kalista and Riondro positioned themselves close to the compound's main laboratories, a highly secured and fortified section of the facility. The last half mile of the trip required them to harness inconspicuously behind the compound's massive walls and grapple a half mile down the ventilation shaft. Their position would make it much easier for Reggie's sensors to tap into and to manipulate the compound's security systems.

When they reached point, Reggie's voice boomed over their communication sets. "It's about time! Are you two okay? I picked up a lot of gunfire."

"We're okay, Reg. What's next?" Riondro asked.

"Give me a second. I did a work-up on your physical traits and found one unusual element. Every time you perform those miraculous feats of yours, it triggers a building response. Your power increases exponentially in crisis mode. And for some reason, Sis, your strengths and abilities have increased by eighty percent— much faster than Riondro's. I can't figure it out, but from what I can tell, it's harmless to you both. You just keep getting better."

"Of course we do." Kalista nudged Riondro. "What's going on in the compound?"

"I have good news and bad news. The good news is that I'm still pretty. The bad news is they've gone on full alert and the guards are set up in a full manual shutdown mode. They put something over that manhole you two used to enter the facility."

"Is there any way of getting to the lab undetected?" she asked.

"Guns blazing seems to be the only way in."

Riondro spoke. "I want you to guide us through every step of the way. If all goes well, we'll exit the way we came in. Can you tell what's on top of the manhole?"

"I don't have a clear read, but it looks like it isn't thick enough to withstand a blast from a couple of bars of C-4. I'm sure it won't pose a problem."

"Good! Clear the line and see if you can find us the quickest route to the labs."

Kalista prepped her arsenal, thoroughly checking her ammunition, grenades, and guns in silence.

Riondro placed a hand on her shoulder. "Just remember why we're here. This is a search and destroy mission that will eradicate the worst strain of cancer mankind has ever known. We are doctors who'll do damn near anything to find a cure. So let's cowboy up and do it!"

She set a fresh clip into her Uzi and looked up at him. "You know, since you came into my life, something is different. I used to walk into the fire without worrying about whether I lived or died. Now I feel like I have something to live for—you, Reggie, and our cause. I want to keep fighting for what I believe is right. And if I die doing that, at least it won't be a selfish death. I feel like I've been preparing for this moment all my life." She shouldered the gun. "Let's do this thing."

* * *

Thirty soldiers stood guard in the hallway beyond the ventilation system.

Reggie's voice crackled over the COM. "There's a storage room about eight feet to your left. Climb down there. After you're in, close the vent. You'll have to blast your way out the door. It's going to be one hell of a coming-out party."

"I see the storage room," Riondro said.

"After you clear this first hurdle, make a sharp right and I'll guide you the rest of the way."

Riondro unhinged the vent and they both climbed down through the duct. Kalista lined the hall door with C-4 explosives and set the timer for thirty seconds. The pair huddled behind a thick steel desk.

The door blew, taking a good chunk of the wall with it and filling the hallway with smoke and concrete dust. In the midst of the carnage, the pair rushed out of the room under the cover of smoke, flames, and dust.

The guards fell back, trying to take cover against the walls. Half of them turned and ran as Riondro rolled out a handful of grenades.

"At the end of the hallway, make a quick right," Reggie said. "They're sending reinforcements, so move it."

They moved steadily through the hallway, creating a barrage of grenades and gunfire as bullets whizzed by. They fired clip after clip, taking out anyone who stood in their way, but the firefight became increasingly difficult as guards piled on. They stood their ground and moved in unison.

Reggie cheered them on. "The lab's around the corner to your right. Get your asses over there while I search for the access codes."

They barreled through the debris in the hallway, their bodies at turns vanishing and reappearing through the flames and smoke. As they rounded the corner, the smoke began to clear and they saw a huge iron door with a digital keypad nestled in an indention in the wall. A door beside the lab entrance opened and they came face-to-face with two heavily armed agents—a man and a woman.

"We got them, sir," Agent Hilton said into her communicator.

"Do yourselves a favor and drop your weapons," Agent Numan said. Kalista and Riondro glanced at each other. Hilton cocked her weapon and glared at them. "Don't even contemplate an escape. There's absolutely no fucking way out of this facility."

Agents Ingro and Tips emerged from the side door.

"There's no one else with you, is there?" Ingro asked, grinning. "What in the fuck were you two expecting to achieve in all this? I advise you to drop your fucking weapons or I'm going to take pleasure in gutting you both."

Reggie's voice came through in their earphones. "Shit, guys, they don't know you've actually taken the serum. Just do what they say! It might buy us some time to figure how to get you two out of this. I've devised a detachment communicator, so when your primary communications are removed they can't trace its origin, because the main beacon's in your ear. I'll still be able to communicate with you both."

Riondro looked into Doug Ingro's eyes. "You son of a bitch."

"You knew my mother, Lieutenant? Stand the fuck down."

"Guys, back off. This fucker's serious," Reggie said.

Three soldiers behind Ingro crouched, guns drawn. Ingro smiled as he motioned to Agent Tips. "Take their weapons."

Kalista and Riondro surrendered their guns, then Tips fell back beside Agent Ingro.

"Kill them both," Ingro said.

Numan and Hilton cocked their weapons, moving closer to Kalista and Riondro.

"Bye-bye, heroes," Numan said with a smile.

"Delay that order!"

From out of nowhere, Walker appeared. Numan and Hilton immediately lowered their weapons and stood at attention.

20

Kalista and Riondro dangled two feet above a basin of water, hanging from ropes tied around their wrists. Armed guards surrounded them from every dark corner. From the underground sanctuary back in New York, Reggie desperately attempted to contact them, but his connection was riddled with static. Pacing the room, Reggie suddenly heard a faint voice filtering in on his speakers. He rushed back to his console and twisted a few knobs to adjust the sound. By rapidly flipping frequencies, he cleared the lines and heard his sister's voice faintly from the speakers.

"Yeah," she said in a whisper. "We're here."

"Thank God!" Reggie said. "I've been trying to contact you both for an hour and a half. What's going on? Is R.B. okay?"

"We're hanging by ropes over water. Off to the side is some sort of an electrical contraption. I figure it's a torture device of some kind. You got any suggestions?"

"Not yet. I detect a group of people on their way to your location. I'm trying my best to get you two the hell out of there, but—"

"But nothing!" She abruptly cut him off. "I know you'll do your best."

*　*　*

Walker, Ingro, Tips, Numan, and Hilton walked through the hallway. Walker stopped in front of the two captives.

"Congratulations on escaping from your mission five years ago," he said. "There's just one thing I need to know before we kill you."

"Fuck you," Riondro returned.

Ingro started toward him, but Walker held out his hand.

"For a man hanging by his last rope, you sure have a mouth full of shit." Behind him, Walker's team chuckled. "Tell me, how did you two get out of that damn jungle during your mission? Better yet, how did you manage to eliminate my soldiers in the sewage lines?"

Reggie's voice came through their earphones. "Guys, I'm picking up major activity outside the compound. Twenty S-70A Black Hawk helicopters, armed to the teeth, about three miles out, closing faster than a motherfucker. These birds are modified like there's no tomorrow. Bunker busters, handheld nuclear devices, all kinds of shit. They're equipped with some sort of weird propulsion system. This is not looking good."

Walker snarled to Ingro. "Fuck this! They're useless to me if they won't talk. Drop them into the tank."

One of the agents released a lever attached to an electrical panel off to the side. Kalista and Riondro were lowered into the basin below them, which immediately sent a charge of electricity through their bodies.

Walker said, "As you may have noticed, I'm not a patient man. I'll just sum up everything I want to know from you." He signaled the agent to bring them up. "Who else out there is connected with you, where in the fuck is George Thimpkin, and what do you know about my fucking project? Answer now, or I assure you, you'll never come back up."

Kalista and Riondro looked at each other and smiled.

"You stupid son of a bitch!" Kalista shouted down to Walker.

"You murderous asshole!" Riondro added.

"You'll never get one motherfucking word out of us—"

"So kiss our asses!"

The pair dissolved into laughter.

Walker placed his hands in his pockets and waited for the laughter to die out. "Lieutenant Buckner," he said, "I hope you had the chance to crack into this sweet piece of ass hanging next to you before you came to my fucking facility in your weak-ass attempts at pissing on my operation. If you won't answer any of my questions, at least tell me this—was the pussy so good you'd follow this stupid bitch to your death? Was it better than your wife's?"

Kalista swung forward and kicked at Walker, her boots barely missing his face.

He stepped back, laughing. "Hey, that was close. You have a little quickness in you! I like my bitches rough around the edges. I'd love to get a whiff of the cunt of the great Captain Kalista Flaker to see if it's true."

"If what's true, you son of a bitch?" Kalista snapped.

"If you have balls like everyone said." He looked at his watch. "Looks like it's time to die. Drop them!" The agent pushed the lever again, lowering Kalista and Riondro into the water, then increased the electrical charge until their bodies jerked and danced from the current. They both screamed in pain, writhing against the ropes.

* * *

Reggie kept trying to communicate with Kalista and Riondro, but again his system was blocked by heavy static. Suddenly, a foreign line activated on his console and a clear voice echoed from the speakers.

"Reggie Flaker, don't be alarmed—we're the good guys. We've been keeping an eye on you and you've done a damn good job. At this point I'll be relieving you of your duties and taking over the operation. We're going in after your sister."

"Shit—" was all Reggie could muster in response.

The signal went dead, leaving Reggie with nothing but static on his monitor. Within a minute the signal again activated and a different voice came through—an older, more refined voice.

"A longtime friend wants to remind you to watch your mouth, young man. Over and out." The line went dead.

* * *

The choppers released a barrage of missiles on the compound, firing in a pre-arranged pattern that did the greatest possible damage. First they hit the compound's satellite communication center and backup generators, then they launched an attack on the runway and the helicopter and jet hangars. They bore down upon the compound with pinpoint accuracy. After this barrage of artillery, soldiers by the dozens came roping from each of the choppers, heading for every opening of the massive Gecko Bravo compound.

* * *

The building trembled and a series of explosions rocked the compound.

Walker spun around. "What the fuck? Everybody out of here! Ingro, find out what the fuck's going on."

"Yes, sir, but what about them?"

"It looks these two weren't alone after all! Pull them out—we may need them as a bartering tool, if they're still alive."

* * *

Minutes or hours passed. Kalista opened her eyes to see General George Thimpkin kneeling down in front of her. He brushed the wet hair from her face and she saw tears streaming from his eyes. *I must be dead*, she thought. *Why is he crying? He should be glad to see I made it to heaven.* She glanced over at Riondro just as he opened his eyes.

"I'll be goddamned!" General Thimpkin stared at them, his mouth hanging open.

Kalista didn't know whether to laugh or cry. "Daddy!" she called.

As Thimpkin cut them loose, Walker charged back into the room and tossed him against the wall. Kalista reacted reflexively, kicking Walker in the chest and sending him back out the door. Ingro, Tips, Numan, and Hilton rushed into the room as Riondro moved to Kalista's side.

"Gung ho?" he asked.

"You're goddamn right!" she responded.

Rubbing his chest, Walker walked back into formation. "How in the fuck did you come back to life?"

"No more questions, you fucking bastard," Kalista said. "We're not strung up anymore. Figure it out for yourself."

"You killed my family!" Riondro said, glaring at Ingro.

Ingro laughed. "I've killed so many people I can't keep track."

Riondro's eyes narrowed. "You ignorant son of a bitch."

"Lieutenant, your rotting family was insignificant to all of us," Walker said. "People like you two sicken me. You think you can save the world? Humanity was born to be led. You can't save them, because they crave our domination. And you idiots spent most of your sorry lives following orders that furthered our cause.

You're no better than I am. Humanity will be led one way or the other, whether it's by you or by people like me. Personally, I prefer me."

Kalista stepped toward him. "I hope those words were your last will and testament, because you're going to die. Are you ready?"

"Am I ready to die? No, bitch, not today."

The Gecko Bravo agents rushed toward Kalista and Riondro, slamming them both against the wall. Their bodies slid down to the floor.

"This is pitiful!" Walker laughed. "With mouths like these two have, I was convinced they had some fight in them." Tips and Numan took the lead, hauling the soldiers up.

"Now!" Riondro shouted. They reached back in unison and twisted their heads until the bones cracked.

Witnessing the brutal execution, Hilton froze in place. Riondro caught her by the back of the neck. "Walker, is this one of your agents, or your bitch?"

Kalista stepped toward her. "You can leave or you can die, princess. It's up to you."

Riondro released Hilton. She turned and glanced at Walker and Ingro before booking out the door.

"She must have been your bitch," Kalista smiled.

Walker frowned, watching Hilton leave. "Ingro, do something with these two, would you please?"

"Your other bitch," Kalista said.

Riondro looked at Kalista. "He's mine."

Walker, watching the hand-to-hand between Riondro and Ingro, was surprised to find himself on the receiving end of a powerful kick from Kalista. She was on him and before he could scream, she disconnected both arms from their sockets with a wrenching move. Arms useless, he tried to scuttle away on his rear, but Kalista caught him up and threw him into the basin. Thimpkin cranked the electrical charge and Walker finally screamed, a high howling sound, as he thrashed in the water.

Thimpkin tossed an Uzi to Riondro, who caught it after crushing Ingro's nose against his boot. He emptied an entire clip into Ingro's head, the powerful weapon chewing up his skull and brain like mincemeat. He sprayed bullets across the room, into each of the agents on the floor, ensuring they would never regenerate.

Kalista shook the general's hand.

"A little rusty?" she asked.

"Bullshit!" Thimpkin brushed himself off. "That was a sucker punch."

"Sucker punch or not, you'd kick my ass from here to Mars if I ever got caught off-guard like that."

"I have a feeling that's not going to happen anytime soon."

Kalista returned his smile. "How many times are you planning to save my life?"

"As long as I have warm blood in my body, soldier."

Kalista introduced the two men in her life to one another.

"The pleasure's all mine, General!" Riondro shook hands with Thimpkin. "I thought for sure you were dead."

"I did too, frankly," Thimpkin said.

"Could you give us a moment, please?" Kalista asked Riondro.

"Of course. I need to secure the area." He touched her shoulder on the way out.

"I see he cares about you," Thimpkin said. With the knuckle of his forefinger, the old general lifted Kalista's chin and looked into her eyes. "I've always been your father and I always will be. Come here, sweetheart, and give me a hug. I've waited too long for this."

Kalista rushed into his arms and buried her face in his shoulder. "I love you so much, Daddy," she whispered.

"And I you, baby girl."

After a while, Thimpkin stepped back and resumed his military bearing. "I've been keeping my eye on you these past five years, and you've done a damn good job, Captain."

"Hooah, General!" responded Kalista with a smile as several of Thimpkin's men rushed into the room.

"Sir, the compound's secure. Here are the lab disks you requested."

"General, you know about this?" Kalista asked.

"More than you know, Captain. These disks will give us a better edge in this fight—that is, if we can decode them."

"You mean it's not over? Walker was babbling all kinds of stuff, but I didn't believe him."

"This conspirators' coup is bigger than you realize. You started a fight against something larger than all of us. Telling the world won't stop their plot, but it's a beginning." Thimpkin put his hand on Kalista's shoulder. "My men were the ones who sent that missile toward my chopper in Vietnam. Your recovery was a mission within a mission for me."

"How are we going to finally stop the conspirators?" Kalista asked.

"Without knowing it, you've been part of a resistance union. We call ourselves Fierce Chicanery—a union forged to take down conspirators by any means necessary."

One of Thimpkin's men ran into the room. "Pardon me, General, but there's something you need to know. We just did blood work on Damion Walker—the person we just killed wasn't him. They don't even have the same blood type."

"Goddammit!" Thimpkin snapped to action. "Gather the men and scour this facility until you find him—and do it fast."

Riondro walked back into the room. "We're all clear. What's the rush?"

"It's Walker," Kalista said. "He's not dead."

Riondro's eyes went to the basin.

"That wasn't him," she said.

Thimpkin spoke. "We have a huge problem on our hands. If Walker escaped, our resistance—The Order—will be exposed and compromised. We need to act now."

Before they could make a move, the lights in the compound went out. Everyone in the room found themselves in a fight for their lives against unknown assailants in total darkness.

21

General Thimpkin knelt on the floor, blindfolded, tied, and gagged with a group of men in black suits and dark glasses standing around him. He had put up a valiant fight in the dark compound but was taken in, a group of shadowy figures grappling his body to the ground. That was weeks ago. After he was captured, the general was transported to an old abandoned warehouse that smelled of sawdust and mold. A single light hung from above with a halogen bulb that warmed the black sheet folded over his head and face.

Through the sheet, he could barely make out a dark figure moving closer to him. He heard the man's shoes click on the floor. He knew the sound of those shoes—standard dress shoes for black ops agents.

From behind, someone removed the blindfold and ripped the gag from his mouth.

Squinting as his eyes adjusted to the light, Thimpkin stared at his captor.

"Walker, you son of a bitch."

Walker smiled. "I'm sure by now you suspect the information disks you stole from my unit were useless. I had a suspicion my unit would be compromised at a crucial moment, so I made certain arrangements. Honestly, I was glad to see that team go. Did you really think we could be stopped, even by the great George Thimpkin?"

Walker screwed a silencer attachment to his handgun and placed the muzzle against Thimpkin's forehead. "We are the definition of conspiracy. I actually want to thank you; with your unexpected raid on the Gecko Bravo compound, you gave us access to Fierce Chicanery. Now, your organization has been exposed and I have all available personnel working overtime to find and destroy your team."

Thimpkin snapped. "You're insane!"

"I prefer to think of it as an edge," Walker said with a smile.

"You think it's over?" Thimpkin asked. "I'm not the heart of Fierce Chicanery. I have many successors, and any one of them could be standing right next to you."

Walker raised an eyebrow at the guard next to him. "This guy?" he asked. "I doubt it. But if you insist." He leveled his weapon at the guard and put a single bullet in the man's head, dropping him.

"You don't have any idea what we're willing to do to make sure murderous fucking psychopaths like you are wiped off the face of this earth," Thimpkin said. "This is not over!"

Walker shook his head. "What a pathetic speech."

Off to the side, one of Walker's agents adjusted his glasses, transmitting an image via concealed fiber optic camera to the headquarters of Fierce Chicanery.

As Walker cocked his weapon, Thimpkin closed his eyes and murmured, "Ask not what your country can do for you—"

Walker pulled the trigger.

* * *

At base camp in a secret location, dozens of Fierce Chicanery agents dressed in black stared at a viewing screen. Kalista, Riondro, and Reggie were present to witness Thimpkin's murder. Without taking their eyes off the screen, everyone spoke in unison: "Ask what you can do for your country."

When the screen went black, everyone turned their attention to the three newest members of Fierce Chicanery. An agent bearing a large package moved through the gathering and made his way toward Kalista. "Major," he said. "The floor is yours."

She stared into space, stunned. "What?" she mumbled.

A tear trickled down Reggie's face. Riondro put his arm around the young man's shoulders.

"Why did this happen?" Kalista said, her voice a dreamy whisper. Her train of thought had chugged to a stop.

Riondro watched her closely. Though the serum had proved beneficial to them both, her strength was ten times that of his own and if she lost control of herself, he feared no one could stop her. She could easily kill everyone in the room.

She narrowed her eyes at the agent standing in front of her with the box. "What the fuck did you say?"

He thrust the box toward her. "The floor is yours. Fierce Chicanery is forged from a bloodline—"

"Don't give me riddles. What the hell is going on here?"

"General Thimpkin chose you as his successor," the agent intoned calmly, "effective upon his death. This fight is just beginning." He placed the box at her feet.

She looked around the room, her eyes burning. "What about General Thimpkin, you sons of bitches? You all stand here looking at me like you all run on fucking batteries. What is wrong with you people?"

"Major, please," the agent said. "Time is of the essence. Hundreds of us here, thousands worldwide, are now at your command. Speaking for The Order of Fierce Chicanery, the decision our general made in choosing you to lead us is most fitting. We'll follow you into hell and back."

* * *

Walker's laughter bounced off the walls of the warehouse. Unscrewing the silencer attachment and holstering his weapon, Walker took hold of the dead man's face, examining the wound. "That's one nasty little hole you got there, General." Somewhere from the shadows of the room, Walker heard a low pulsing beep.

At that moment, Fierce Chicanery's imbedded agent received a transmission from headquarters. "The device has been activated. You have approximately three minutes. Your service and sacrifice will not be in vain."

"Affirmative!" the agent said in a whisper too low to be detected by normal humans. Walker looked directly at the agent.

"Agents!" he yelled.

The imbedded agent was disarmed of all weaponry. Unarmed, he assumed protocol position before Walker and his men.

"Who are you?" Walker asked.

"I'm not at liberty to say."

Walker smiled. "You people are everywhere! Fucking termites. I will find great pleasure in seeking every one of you out." He got close enough for the optics to get a good look. "Whoever's watching out there? Your days are numbered. I won't stop until you kneel before me."

He grabbed the imbedded agent by his throat, ripping out his larynx. Embedded in the throat cavity, he found small metallic container. Walker wasn't familiar with the exact type of bomb, but from his experience he knew the smaller the deadlier.

Sensing that the device was close to detonating, he immediately hurled the object upward like a bullet, sending it crashing through a skylight and a little over a half mile into the night sky. Within seconds the device detonated, lighting up the sky and shaking the earth's foundation.

On the ground, Walker's agents were blown off their feet and momentarily blinded by the intense light from the explosion as the blast disintegrated the rooftop. Pockets of lit debris dripped onto the ground like trails of burst fireworks.

Walker, standing his ground, was unfazed by the ferocity of the enormous blast. He didn't even blink. Walker's agents were taken back—not only by the intensity of the explosion, but by the unbelievable abilities their boss demonstrated. He sensed their fear and laughed at it.

"What are you?" asked one of the agents. He pointed his weapon at Walker, but the pistol shook uncontrollably.

"Unfortunately, what you all just witnessed is highly classified," Walker said. "I can't let you out of here alive."

"Take him out!" the agent cried. The men emptied and reloaded clip after clip into Walker until they drained their ammo.

Walker withstood the barrage, bullet-tattered clothing dangling from his body in shreds, with a sinister smile on his face. "Are you done?" he asked, once the ammo was exhausted. Tearing away his shirt and jacket, he laughed in the men's faces as his open wounds healed before their eyes.

"Didn't you know?" Walker taunted them. "I'm a God!" He sped around the room like a bolt of lightning, ripping the men to pieces with his hands.

Dropping the bloody flesh-covered torso of one of the agents, Walker felt something ominous in the air. Thimpkin stood and confronted Walker—the hole in his head a mere memory.

"I'll be damned!" Walker said.

Thimpkin's voice was strained and distorted. "You were damned when you sold your soul to a species that's been using you to further their objective."

"What about you, you fucking hypocrite!"

"Sorry, try again. The man you recognize as General George Thimpkin died the moment you pierced his cranium with that archaic little weapon of yours. I inherited his body and his memories. My species, the Cel'jul, have been at war with the Voli' for time beyond your comprehension. The Voli' implanted a seed in your brain, and when this seed hatched, you became a Pas'ool. In your language, you are a bug, a pet of the Voli'."

"Fuck you! I'm nobody's pet! Thanks to Aneman, I am a God!"

"You believe that this Aneman serum you had injected into your bloodstream—a simple serum you humans contrived—gives you the abilities you've demonstrated?" Thimpkin shook his head. "You animals say you want peace on earth and good will toward men, but you long for death and destruction. Your species prays for peace on earth, then invent heinous methods of torture and slaughter. Your kind conceived of napalm bombs, torture, gas chambers, flame-throwers, concentration camps, and AIDS—a biological weapon forged by secretive individuals such as yourself, Walker. You think you've invented something great, experimenting with what you don't comprehend, when in fact you've played right into the hands of a more intelligent species. The seed inside you feeds on the act of death and destruction."

"Why in the fuck are you telling me all this?"

"Seeing as time is of the essence, I'll get right to the point: a proposition, Walker! Allow me to remove the Pas'ool. Never has my species been able to retrieve a living sample for experimentation."

"If you're so powerful, why don't you take it from me?"

"The carrier of the Pas'ool must submit willingly."

"What if I don't give it up?"

"Then you must perish, as carrier of the Voli'."

"I've never been one to submit to anything and I'm not about to start now."

"Very well," Thimpkin said. The general's body dropped heavy to the floor and within seconds, Walker was surrounded by dozens of unearthly creatures. Their physical forms were so advanced that his mind could not comprehend them. They appeared to him as beacons of light.

Walker fell to his knees, holding his stomach in pain. Paralyzed, he shuddered as one of the creatures moved toward him.

A voice entered his mind. "Good boy!"

"Fuck you!" Walker struggled to return.

"You have passed our test, human. We watched as that filthy Cel'jul attempted to sway you. You carry within you our beloved Pas'ool."

"If you are Voli', let me go, goddammit." He was immediately released from the intense pain. Swiftly standing, he prepared himself for a fight.

"Heel, my pet."

Against his will, Walker's fists unclenched and he stood at attention, an obedient dog to his master.

"Stop fucking playing with me, you son of a bitch!" he managed to growl. "If you're going to kill me, hurry the fuck up and get it over with already."

"There's no need to be suicidal. You carry within you a precious gift of our species. Killing you would be asinine. We only want to assist you in reaching your objective—creating that new world order you and many others like you speak of daily. You, sir, are who we've chosen to lead this new world, not those, who for years have ordered you to map out its success. Monitoring over a project that neither one of you has been able to fully understand— carrying out cloaked operations from the shadows of your societies. We will help you build your military."

* * *

With a sigh, Kalista took a moment to regain her composure after her fiery outburst. "My apologies to you, sir," she said to the agent. She turned to everyone else in the room. "To you all. I apologize."

"Apologies are not necessary," the agent said. "If you will follow me, a stateroom awaits you. The review of the confidential information before you is for your eyes only."

"Go!" Riondro said. Hesitating for only a moment more, Kalista followed the agent.

* * *

Coming up on a door, the agent asked Kalista to touch the door and to say Thimpkin's full name.

The door opened. As they entered, the room spoke to them—a soft female's voice.

"Welcome, Major, I've been expecting you. I'm picking up the presence of agent 1-781. Moderate stress level confirmation required. Agent will be terminated if not confirmed in approximately three seconds —three—two—"

"Confirmed!" Kalista said.

"Confirmation accepted. The eagle is watching."

Kalista looked at the agent curiously.

"That means I'm being watched very closely, Major. I'm sure everything will become clearer to you the further you get into all this. You have eighteen of these staterooms around the world, seventeen of which nobody in The Order knows the whereabouts. The general called it a necessary evil. As you can see from the array of personal effects, this particular stateroom was the one he called home."

"Thank you, Mr.—"

The agent placed the box on the desk. She noticed that the box had a coded entry, but looked nothing like the combination pad on the box she had been given in Vietnam. Another riddle. "My name is Agent Richard Portman Jacks—identification code 1-781."

"Thank you, Agent Jacks."

"The pleasure's all mine, Major. If you need anything at all, two agents assigned to your stateroom are at your service."

"One last thing," she said. "As far as I know I wasn't promoted to Major prior to my abrupt departure from the Corps."

Agent Jacks nodded. "The promotion in rank for both you and Lieutenant Commander Buckner might not seem clear at the moment and possibly for months to come, your work against the Aneman Project made heroes out of you. Your honors are well-deserved."

With a salute, Agent Jacks left Kalista alone in the stateroom.

* * *

In the hallway, Jacks was immediately greeted by another agent—his sense of urgency evident in his approach.

"Was the mission successful?" Jacks asked.

"No, sir. You'll have to see the damage for yourself." The agent tapped a clipboard nervously.

"What is it?"

"Sir, the shroud has been breached. The Voli' have found a successful host for their Pas'ool."

"And this host would be?"

"It's Walker, sir."

Horror flashed on Jacks's face. "What makes you say this?"

"Sir, the sector has just informed me that they've been directly contacted by the Cel'jul."

* * *

The stateroom was practically a museum to the life of Kalista's mentor, friend, and father figure. She walked slowly through the room, gazing at photographs of Thimpkin with presidents, dictators, and congressmen from around the world. Souvenirs from far-flung lands graced his bookshelves. Behind a thin plate of glass, thousands of neatly arranged folders were coded in an unusual written language.

The characters seemed hieroglyphic in nature, but they were far from the pictorial symbols used in ancient Egypt. Kalista found all of it ominously beautiful.

She picked up a framed photograph of Thimpkin, Reggie, and herself. The photograph was taken on her eighteenth birthday when Thimpkin had bought time on a charter boat for a private party with just the three of them. The tears began to flow as she hugged the frame to her chest. The three had gone fishing that morning and the day ended with her catching an eight-pound bass. The photo depicted one of the first times in her young life when she actually felt happy. Wiping away her tears, she put down the picture and took a seat at Thimpkin's desk. She felt like a kid in the big leather chair. Before her, she found a folder. On front, stamped in dark black letters, she read:

CLASSIFIED—VIEW FIRST

Some are convinced that America is the champion of freedom, but hidden behind the concept of freedom is an ingeniously forged truth.

* * *

LIVE YOUR LIFE AS IT HAS BEEN METICULOUSLY CON-STRUCTED—FOLLOW AND TRUST YOUR GOVERNMENT WITHOUT QUESTION OR RESISTANCE— OR ELSE THE ASSASSINATION OF JOHN F. KENNEDY AND

*THE STRATEGIC MOVE MADE ON SEPTEMBER 11TH WILL
NOT BE YOUR ONLY EXAMPLES OF OUR SUPREME RULE!*

* * *

*FREEDOM IS IDEAL, BUT FEAR PACKS A GREATER
PUNCH!*

* * *

Kalista found this type of rhetoric extremely odd coming
from a proven soldier like Commander Thimpkin. She continued
on; if she was to honor his death by following his final orders, she
meant to do so without pause. Kalista buried herself in the document,
intent on understanding what she considered her biggest mission
ever. This mission, like all missions she undertook throughout her
military career, she planned on successfully following out to its end.

* * *

Dear Kalista,

*If you're reading this, I've fallen in an ongoing war that I
subsequently chose you to continue the fight far into the future. Wipe
those tears, soldier, and bury your ass into what I've left for you. You'll
find a wealth of information that you must comprehend in order to
perform the job at hand. The information contained in this document,
along with the other materials in your possession, are for your eyes only.*

*It is imperative that you keep this information secure, guarding
it with not only your life, but also in the case of your death.*

*The Roswell, UFO incident of 1947 was a day that will go down
in infamy in the minds of anyone who has ever contemplated the notion
that we are not alone. Multiple credible witnesses believe a number of*

flying saucers actually crash-landed in Roswell and were recovered by the government under a thick shroud of secrecy.

Because these claims lack "hard" evidence, they're typically dismissed. But based on the plethora of eyewitness accounts and the initially clumsy lies from military officials, the Roswell incident of 1947 has become one of the most thoroughly documented investigations on record.

Evidence tells of another crash site, in an area near Socorro, New Mexico. A witness discovered the wreckage of a metallic disc resting on the ground with bodies strewn around. The first witness on this scene was Grady L. "Barney" Barnett, a civil engineer with the United States Soil Conservation Service who was on a military assignment at the time. He relayed the story to some friends in early July 1947. He said the metallic disk was about twenty-five to thirty feet in diameter. While he was examining it, a small group of people arrived on the scene who stated they were part of an archaeological research team from the University of Pennsylvania.

It was said that Mr. Barnett was never interviewed concerning details of his account.

This was not true.

Mr. Barnett was interviewed by my father—Four-star General Henry C. Thimpkin—while Thimpkin was a three-star general with the Army. My father kept the results of this interview to himself because he was the leader of a secret society known as Fierce Chicanery—the very same society you now lead. And to answer your question, yes; secrecy is a necessary evil meant to protect you and those closest to you.

In his account of what he saw upon arriving at the site in Socorro, Mr. Barnett said he witnessed the wreckage of a metallic disk resting on the ground, with several unearthly bodies in the area. On the other side of a ridge he found eight badly injured non-humanoids. One of the beings hobbled toward him, handed him a small metallic sphere, and pleaded with him to insert that object inside the ship. After doing so, Mr. Barnett discovered six teenagers.

These humanoids seemingly appeared from nowhere after he inserted the spherical object into the ship. The non-humanoids were nowhere to be seen. They informed the suspicious Mr. Barnett that they were part of an archaeological research team from the University of Pennsylvania. After that, Mr. Barnett experienced a blinding flash and awoke at the site hours later with only a partial memory of what happened. Witnesses who arrived after the fact saw indications that something large had been in the area.

With each passing day, Mr. Barnett found himself remembering more of what took place that day. Unfortunately, his story became increasingly unbelievable and, in time, he was considered an unreliable witness. Those who knew "Barney" Barnett described him as a respectable and honest citizen—not someone likely to invent such a fantastic tale.

After a painstaking investigation into the university's research and development and archaeological departments, it was established that the university was involved in archaeological digs near the Socorro area at the time. Incidentally, Socorro is about one hundred fifty miles west of Brazel's ranch.

* * *

As he entered into his last days in presidential office, Dwight Eisenhower needed to get something off his chest, something that was and still is of utmost importance: Eisenhower knew that for generations upon generations, an experiment would affect America and the world. After his death, the development of Project Aneman was finally realized, and a superhuman armed force was created. Eisenhower was a family man and naturally feared that this bold project, among many others, would eventually affect his own people.

Like all American politicians and presidents in particular, Eisenhower was deeply embedded in a tight spiritual manacles forged by cloaked deviants within a secret collective. Therefore, he couldn't say much to warn America or the world of what was happening. However, he did try.

Supposedly for the sake of strengthening our national security, this world of mad science was given a green light long ago. Genetic and nuclear scientists are given free access to produce results. These scientists regularly experiment in advanced nuclear arms, chemical warfare, genetic and synthetic robotics, DNA manipulation, cloning, and much more. To aid their inhumane practices, these mad scientists routinely order the abduction of human beings for the purpose of experimentation. Everyday citizens are randomly abducted by the thousands and cut up like lab rats. Given the nature of their work, many of these scientists are naturally conditioned to fear for their own lives along with the lives of their families, and anyone they've ever known.

Today's advanced experiments focus on drastic human evolution. Nationwide lab tests are so broad that even our daily food sources—from seed to grocery shelf—are genetically altered. This is the result of the unholy alliance between the FDA and the multibillion-dollar drug companies, which wish only to please their shareholders and to profit at any cost. Illness on a massive scale is no obstacle to their greed.

New medications are tested on a nationwide scale. They're taken out of the labs—after all, animal testing tells scientists only so much—and introduced directly to the American public.

But there's something even scarier: the drug companies are also in league with corrupt, high-ranking officials throughout the political arena. In the process, new FDA-approved drugs hit the market, followed by massive advertising campaigns. Americans, lured in by the hype, believe the FDA endorsements and essentially volunteer as lab rats. In less than a year's time, these same drugs leave a trail of dead bodies, cancer patients, suicides, and more.

Back to our nation's 34th president. Eisenhower witnessed extraterrestrial bodies recovered after the Roswell incident. Like presidents over the years, he was fully aware of the early stages of Project Aneman and was set against its further development. The development Mr. Eisenhower so opposed—vehemently and ultimately futilely— eventually led America to its role in the grandest science experiment the world would know—an experiment which placed the American soldier in a goddamn test tube.

Project Aneman was the primary reason America set out to invade Vietnam. Though Eisenhower tried to stop it, his authority meant nothing to the powers that truly rule America. Ultimately, his hands were tied when it came to telling the American public about the UFO phenomenon. However, in his final days as commander in chief, he chose to covertly warn us about this massive plot. He specifically instructed the public to beware of the military-industrial complex.

America isn't the only country with extraterrestrial DNA and technology. Unbeknownst to anyone, the entire world has been long embroiled in the midst of a worldwide race.

Now, open the scope up and look beyond the world. Our universal brethren have set their plan into overdrive by allowing mankind to do what comes naturally: self-destruction. They've long cloaked their plan behind crop circles and UFO sightings, always only hinting at their keen knowledge of humanity's drive for absolutism.

We've never been alone. In this intergalactic chess game we are only the pieces. We're taught that America is a democratic society founded for the people, but in reality, this nation has always been a bureaucracy run by the unelected.

It began in Roswell and continued like a dark thread in the tapestry of American culture. This thread passed unnoticed through Vietnam, Aneman, and even the assassination of President Kennedy.

There were many motivations behind President Kennedy's assassination: his choice to go against the corrupt political grain of past administrations; his outspoken stance against the existence of secret societies; his desire for drastic social change. Another card was tipped in his interview with reporter Bill Holden on Air Force One. Holden asked Kennedy in 1963 what he thought about UFOs. The president was very serious when he replied, "I'd like to tell the public about the alien situation, but my hands are tied."

In the end, Project Aneman—our government's pet project that sprung up after the UFO incident in Roswell—happened to be the sharpened sword that ultimately ended his life.

* * *

This very moment, I bet you're asking yourself why? This one-word question is one that many of us first learn and continue to use throughout our lives.

The Order has used the concept of alternative history to slowly awaken the masses to the covert doings of individuals of this world and beyond. It's a weapon stronger than you may think, for one cannot save a world nestled in a box, strategically dormant to the realities of their existence.

By exposing the masses to the idea of an alternative history, it will help to soften the blow felt when the world's dirty laundry can no longer be contained. And when this dirty laundry is exposed, a universal resistance, like nothing ever witnessed in the history of this planet, will rise to fight.

In reading this, you may find my writing completely out of character, especially given that it's coming from a dedicated Corpsman such was myself, but you must first understand that true patriotism means having the strength and will to weed through the bullshit—of a society, a nation, a government—and then speak the truth. Patriotism is at its best when an American constructively and artistically displays decency with valor. Being that America is supposedly of the people, by the people, and for the people, it must be the people who rise up.

Kalista, when it comes to the subject of our country, truth is the most complex enigma.

* * *

Behind Roswell, the Kennedy assassination, and the war in Vietnam lies a vast conspiracy wrapped within an enigma. Even Desert Storm and Operation Iraqi Freedom have ties. These larger touchstones represent only a few.

Consider the information in this file nothing but a prelude. Before you get started, I order you to get your head out of your ass. No information I divulge will come close to the following piece you are to burn into your memory and follow religiously: TRUST NO ONE!

22

The first day of 2004 was beautiful—a blue sky dotted with white clouds above the chilly Colorado Mountains. Nestled in the snow-peaked mountains sat a secluded cabin with smoke curling from the chimney.

Kalista and Riondro lay together on the bed, still sweaty and breathing hard from lovemaking. She lay with her head on his chest and he gently caressed her shoulder, humming the theme song from Cheers.

Kalista started singing the lyrics.

Sometimes you want to go
Where everybody knows your name
And they're always glad you came

Riondro joined in.

You want to be where you can see
Our troubles are all the same
You want to go where everybody knows your name

She sighed. "I miss Hanna. She didn't deserve to die that way. All she wanted to do was to live out her golden years. I made that possible for her, at least financially, but I should've found a way to protect her. I could have done more."

"There you go again," he said.

"What do you mean?"

"Blaming yourself for everything that happens. Kicking yourself for shit you can't change."

She sighed. "I know—"

He tickled her in the ribs. "Well, since you know so much, are you going to shut the fuck up now with your worries? Hell, we just got through making love—better yet, you just got through making love to the man of all men—King Dingaling."

"You're stupid!"

"Everybody has a handicap. You'd better be glad mine isn't down there."

She grabbed his balls. "I bet you're going to stop now, aren't you?"

"Easy, don't mess with the family jewels." He laughed as she tightened her grip. "Okay, okay, okay, I'll stop, baby—I'll stop."

"You're serious?"

He tried to quit laughing. "Yes, I'm serious."

She released his balls. They curled up together on the bed, lost in the moment.

He sighed happily. "This cabin was a great idea."

"I'll say!"

"Happy New Year?"

"I think it will be." She traced zigzag lines through the hair on his chest, her mind distant. "But Thimpkin was right—this is just the beginning. Walker was right, too."

"Why do you say that?"

"Think about it. We've told America and the entire world what we know and what we've seen, short of exposing our own enhanced abilities. Otherwise we'd end up as lab rats for NASA. Even Fierce Chicanery doesn't know the truth about us, though we're now essential players in The Order. But did anyone out there really listen to us? Did they care that a radical conspiracy was trying to take over the world? Did they even want to know?"

"It's only been a little under six months since the operation at the Gecko Bravo compound and less than two months since we shared what little we discovered with the world. We did a damn good job, and what we started will be around for years to come. Give it time to sink in. Shit, we haven't even clicked on that television to see what's happening in the world. Don't jump to conclusions."

"But you have to wonder if Walker was right. Humanity was born to be led."

"Have patience. Walker is a psychopath, Hitler times twenty. Don't believe a word he says." He held her for a moment, looking out the window. "Kalista?"

"Hmm?"

"Does that mean you're giving up?"

"Are you fucking kidding me? I'm a rotten apple in a barrel full of fresh fruit."

"What are you saying?"

"That one rotten apple infects everything. Eventually, people will stop and pay attention. Until then, it's just as Thimpkin said— we're public enemy number one! But I'm a true goddamn patriot and I dare anyone to take that title from me."

"Now, that's sexy as hell, my dear." Riondro said, pulling her into a kiss.

Reggie burst into the room, dressed in waders and a t-shirt and carrying three large bass on a stringer. Startled, Kalista and Riondro each grabbed their guns and pointed them at Reggie.

Reggie swung the fish in front of him. "Easy, twin Rambos!"

He strutted over to the kitchen area and dropped the fish into a cooler. "I caught these babies right outside the back door."

He grabbed the television remote off the nightstand and jumped into bed with them, nestling himself in the middle. "Oh, am I interrupting something?"

On TV, an anchorwoman on a 24 hour news channel was speaking urgently into the camera.

"—After what developed recently, many people wonder, worldwide, if in fact this New Year means anything beyond darkness. Could Americans be involved in a massive conspiracy to seize and occupy humanity? Would these conspirators do anything to further their objective—even kill their own citizens in massive numbers—all for power, money, and control?

"Many believe this is the beginning of World War Three—a war of religion, of dominance and political gain. Some say oil has always been the motivation behind President George W. Bush's unyielding stand on terrorism, sparked by the fall of the Twin Towers.

"How could terrorists cause so much damage without inside help? The same question arises with the epidemic of drug trafficking and the problem with illegal aliens spilling over our borders. Though important pieces of the overall story are missing, we now understand the possibilities behind these important and troubling questions. Humanity is now asking the questions and aggressively seeking answers.

"It's like something out of a science fiction movie. Aliens, DNA splicing, developing super-soldiers for the sole purpose of a global takeover. And three lone rangers who risked everything to bring this conspiracy to light: Major Kalista Flaker, Lieutenant Commander Riondro Buckner, and Major Flaker's younger brother, Reginald Milwaukee Flaker, all of whom recently received the distinguished Medal of Honor for their patriotism."

A screen behind the reporter showed footage of the National Security's Gecko Bravo Branch, grounds swarming with news helicopters and civilians with cameras and notebooks.

"One thing is very clear: our elected leaders have chosen for America a new, more aggressive path, both in foreign policy and domestic restructuring. Is this the right path for our nation?

"This New Year will bring new truths for the entire world to contemplate. On this first day of 2004, I wish you all a year of extraordinary discovery in a world that now seems to be unraveling with hidden realities. This has been a special New Year's Day report—"

Riondro switched off the television as all three of them sat up in bed, their backs against the headboard.

"See, Kalista, we're not completely ignored."

"Yeah, I see."

"We were on TV!" Reggie said.

Someone knocked at the front door. Kalista and Riondro reached for their guns again while Reggie tumbled out of bed to answer. Standing before him was a man in black, holding a yellow laminated card with a black dot in the center. Reggie sighed and grabbed the card, which evaporated in his hand.

"You guys should find a better way to announce yourselves," Reggie said. "This is too weird, don't you think?"

The man stared at him without responding.

"Plus, you need to work on your interpersonal skills, you know?" He turned to shout back into the cabin. "Sister soldier! It's for you."

Riondro and Kalista appeared beside Reggie.

"Major." The agent saluted.

"Agent." Kalista nodded.

"Target acquired." The agent spoke into his headset.

Within seconds, from every direction, ten S-70A Black Hawk helicopters surrounded the cabin. Once the helicopters touched down, swarms of agents immediately set up a tight perimeter around. Agent Jacks came hurriedly from out of the lead chopper.

"What's so pressing, Jacks?" Kalista asked. "I'm not sure you noticed, but I'm on vacation with my family."

"Worldwide communications have been tapped, even our arsenal of well-encrypted firewalls have been hacked. Communications have been severed and a pending message is forthcoming. Ma'am, as of forty-five minutes ago, FC-section communications around the globe have been severed."

"Has any intel been hacked?" Riondro asked.

"Luckily, that firewall held and nothing was lost. The intelligence behind this worm has thrown us. We've never been violated in this manner before."

"And how long has this message been pending?" Kalista asked.

Jacks looked at his watch. "Approximately one hour and ten minutes, ma'am. We would have mobilized to you sooner, but I'm sure you understand our need for caution."

"I understand."

"This message," Riondro asked. "Have you been able to configure its origins?"

"That's partly the reason we're here. We need your brother for this one. Our arsenal of systems analysts can't seem to configure or begin to figure out what this worm is comprised of or of how it was manifested."

"Well no kidding," Reggie said.

The agent coughed awkwardly. "If anybody can find a way of locating the source of this worm, we feel and hope that you can, sir." A line of men streamed from the chopper, carrying with them a huge amount of computer equipment.

"Nice setup," Reggie said as the men came in. "Are we playing Counterstrike this time?"

"Even though we're at a loss as to what this incoming message is, finding the source is priority, if we're going to either capture or eliminate the individuals who could have penetrated our global FC-sections, not to mention worldwide security sections."

"Let me get this straight," Kalista said. "As of a little over an hour ago, worldwide communications have been frozen?"

"Affirmative, ma'am. Currently, the world is at the whim of this hacker. And there's no telling how long the planet could be held hostage. As I speak, the United States military has mobilized in every state as Congress and the current presidential administration are contemplating declaring martial law. Every nation in the world is on the brink of unrest."

"Are these nations contemplating nuclear options?"

"Luckily, nuclear activation has proven to be an impossible avenue for any nation. All systems have been compromised. These hackers are sending a clear message that they are in control. Civilian air travel has been halted and the skies now belong solely to the military even though they're flying blind."

"I understand," Kalista said.

"What are your orders, Major?"

Kalista turned to gaze at her vacation safehouse. Inside, Reggie was already advising the men on the proper placement of satellites. She turned her attention back to Jacks. "Are the FC-sections fully secure?"

"We've taken every measure to assure that."

"I take it that a perimeter has been established around our current location and fortified tenfold?"

"Affirmative."

Inside, one of the agents handed Reggie a ham sandwich. Another, clearly working on orders, switched TV stations for the young man. "We can't get shit on this thing," Reggie said. "Every channel shows a picture of a hand with the world rotating on the palm."

Motioning Jacks close, Kalista whispered, "I'm sure you know my brother's unorthodox methods and nerve-wrenching disposition."

"Yes, ma'am."

"If you want to use him you'll have to practice tolerance. Am I making myself absolutely clear?"

"Of course."

"Of course what?"

"Of course, ma'am."

Kalista cinched her robe around her waist and kissed her brother on the forehead. "Stinky, Agent Jacks will be briefing you on this operation. You are to pay close attention to what he has to say, all right?"

"You know me!" Reggie wrapped his arm around the agent's shoulder. "Me and my old wrinkled subordinate here will be just fine—right, Jackie boy?"

A wave of frustration spread across Agent Jacks's face. "Yes sir," he said.

"Reggie, this is important. I need you to be serious about this one, okay?"

"Sure, sis. Does this mean I'm one of your agents now?"

"Hell no!" Kalista said, shutting the bathroom door behind her.

Agent Jacks worked up a smile. "What's that term you seem to use frequently, young man—burned?"

"I thought your old ass loved me, Jacks."

"We're burning time here. Someone out there thinks they know more than you of the ins and outs of a computer. I can't wait to see how you maneuver your way around this particular worm."

"Mr. Jacks, worms are my specialty."

"Let's hope so because this one, at present, is holding the world hostage."

* * *

Reggie worked feverishly, attempting to bypass the heavily encrypted firewalls surrounding this worm, but to no avail. Never has anything been so difficult for this young man to bypass, but he continued on—exhausting every capable brain cell he had focused on this task. An hour flew by as Reggie worked, when a message flashed across the screen:

* * *

HACKERS WORKING FOR THE U.S. GOVERNMENT AND BEYOND ARE ATTEMPTING TO FIND ME AND UNDERSTAND HOW IS IT THAT I COULD HAVE MANAGED TO SHUT DOWN THE ENTIRE WORLD.

YOU'VE PIQUED MY INTEREST! YOUR METHODS ARE QUITE INTRIGUING! YOU'VE COME CLOSER THAN ANY AT CUTTING THROUGH THE FORTIFIED FIREWALLS THAT SURROUND MY SWEET LITTLE WORM.

WHOEVER YOU ARE, KNOW THAT MY INTENTIONS ARE AS NOBLE AS MY LOVE OF COUNTRY. I'M AN AMERICAN PATRIOT ON A MISSION TO AWAKEN HUMANITY TO THE CORRUPTION PLAGUING THIS WORLD AND BEYOND.

I AM AN ESSENTIAL MEMBER OF AN ORGANIZATION FUNDED BY AN ABUNDANCE OF AMERICA'S WEALTH, PRIMARILY FROM THE HIDDEN TREASURES OF THE CONFEDERACY. THE ORGANIZATION I SPEAK OF IS A TENURED ORGANIZATION THAT COVERTLY INFILTRATED THE KNIGHTS OF THE GOLDEN CIRCLE DURING AMERICA'S CIVIL WAR. THE KNIGHTS OF THE GOLDEN CIRCLE IS AN ORGANIZATION FOUNDED BY NONE OTHER THAN THE INFAMOUS JESSE JAMES.

JESSE JAMES FAKED HIS ASSASSINATION, FIRST TO CUT OFF ANY TRACE THAT WOULD POSSIBLY LEAD AUTHORITIES TO STOLEN GOODS, BUT THEN TO TAKE HIS NEW JOB. HE LED THE KNIGHTS OF THE GOLDEN CIRCLE UNDER ASSUMED NAMES UNTIL HE DIED IN THE EARLY 20TH CENTURY!

AS UNBELIEVABLE AS THIS MAY SOUND TO YOU, AN INTERGALACTIC WAR HAS BEEN IN PLAY BETWEEN TWELVE SPECIES OF EXTRATERRESTRIAL RACES SINCE THE BEGINNING OF OUR EXISTENCE ON THIS PLANET. MOREOVER, HUMANITY—EARTHLINGS, IF I MAY—ARE CAUGHT IN THE MIDDLE OF THIS WAR.

THE ABUNDANCE OF UFO SIGHTINGS WE ENCOUNTER DAILY ARE SIGNS OF THIS WAR. AND ITS CHAIN OF EVENTS TRAVELS A LINE ALL THE WAY TO THE WHITE HOUSE. THESE ARE THE REASONS OUR GOVERNMENT SPARES NO EXPENSE AND AGGRESSIVELY SEEKS TO DOUSE THE FLAMES OF UFO SIGHTINGS, ABDUCTIONS, AND ENCOUNTERS. THIS IS A WAR MADE OBVIOUS DUE TO THE ANOMALOUS OCCURRENCES HUMANITY REFERS TO AS MYSTERIES: FROM CROP CIRCLES TO ABDUCTIONS, NOT TO MENTION THE BAFFLING OCCURRENCES STILL TAKING PLACE IN AREAS LIKE KECKSBURG, ROSWELL, GULF BREEZE, AND RENDLESHAM.

THERE WAS AN EARTHLY HABITAT FORGED OF A PEOPLE A VERY LONG TIME AGO THAT WERE HUMAN IN APPEARANCE, BUT IN FACT EXTRATERRESTRIAL. TO THIS DAY, THIS SPECIES LIVES AMONG US, BREEDING WITH HUMANITY AND CREATING OBEDIENT SEEDS— SEEDS THAT HAVE INFILTRATED EVERY FACTION OF OUR WORLD, FROM HOUSEHOLDS TO GOVERNMENTS. WHAT I'M DESCRIBING TO YOU IS AN INVASION—

ONE THAT CANNOT BE STOPPED. THIS SAME SPECIES DESTROYED THE ONCE INHABITED PLANET MARS. THIS SPECIES—A ROGUE ELEMENT AMONG ITS OWN KIND—WERE BANISHED, SENT AWAY FROM ITS HOME WORLD AND FORCED TO BE THE FIRST OF THE SPECIES TO FORGE AN EARTHLY BASE: ATLANTIS.

OUR COUNTRY'S INFAMOUS MAJESTIC 12, WHICH CAME TOGETHER AFTER THE ROSWELL INCIDENT— THEY WERE NOT HUMAN BEINGS. IN ADDITION, PROJECT BLUE BOOK WAS AN INGENIOUS SHROUD TRUMPED UP BY CERTAIN HEADS OF THE UNITED STATES GOVERNMENT TO CONFUSE PROMINENT UFO RESEARCHERS SO THEY WOULD SPOUT FALSE PROPAGANDA. THIS IN TURN CREATED GOVERNMENT PLANTS SENT TO SPREAD DISINFORMATION. I'M THE ONE WHO RELEASED THE MAJESTIC 12 DOCUMENTS AND THE DOCUMENTS ARE, WITHOUT ANY DOUBT, GENUINE IN EVERY FORM AND NEED TO BE ACTED UPON EXPEDITIOUSLY.

SIXTEEN MEMBERS OF THE CURRENT UNITED STATES' PRESIDENTIAL ADMINISTRATION AND FOUR MEMBERS OF CONGRESS ARE LITERALLY NOT OF THIS WORLD. IN ADDITION, AMERICA IS NOT THE ONLY COUNTRY INFILTRATED; IT'S WORLDWIDE.

I'M WARNING YOU ALL THAT THIS SPECIES DOESN'T HAVE HUMANITY'S BEST INTERESTS AT HEART. HUMAN BEINGS ARE THEIR PRIMARY FOOD SOURCE AND THIS HAS BEEN TRUE SINCE THE BEGINNING OF OUR EXISTENCE HERE ON THIS PLANET.

THE PLANET MARS WAS ONCE AS FRUITFUL AND HABITABLE AS EARTH. IT WAS A PLANET OUR ANCESTORS REFERRED TO AS HOME UNTIL THIS

PARTICULAR EXTRATERRESTRIAL RACE INVADED IN A MASSIVE STRIKE THAT NEARLY WIPED OUR SPECIES FROM THE UNIVERSE, UNTIL THREE OTHER EXTRATERRESTRIAL SPECIES CAME TO HUMANITY'S AID. TAKING DNA FROM SURVIVORS OF THE ATTACK, THESE THREE SPECIES SEEDED OUR PLANET.

SOME EXTRATERRESTRIALS FEEL THAT WE MAY BE ABLE TO OFFER THE UNIVERSE AND ITS INHIBITORS MANY THINGS. OTHERS BELIEVE WE LONG FOR DEATH AND DESTRUCTION, GIVEN OUR WARRING NATURE. STILL OTHERS BELIEVE THE HUMAN RACE SHOULD NOT BE ALLOWED TO ADVANCE TO THE POINT WHERE SPACE TRAVEL BECOMES COMMONPLACE.

THE TYPE OF MASSIVE STRIKE INITIATED AGAINST MARS IS NOW MORE DIFFICULT FOR THEM TO INITIATE, DUE TO THE AFOREMENTIONED INTERGALACTIC WAR. BUT TRUST THAT OUR WILLINGNESS TO PARTNER WITH THIS PARTICULAR SPECIES IS NOT WISE. WHAT THEY'RE COLLECTIVELY DOING IS NOT IN THE BEST INTERESTS OF OUR PLANET OR FOR HUMANITY IN GENERAL. YOU HAVE BEEN WARNED.

FOR NOW, I BID YOU A FOND FAREWELL, BUT KNOW THAT THERE'S MORE GOING ON HERE. PAY ATTENTION TO EVERYTHING THAT'S GOING ON IN OUR SOCIETY, FOR WITHIN LIE HIDDEN TRUTHS YOU ARE NOT MEANT TO KNOW. SOON, I WILL INFORM THE MASSES OF THESE TRUTHS AND LET THE CARDS FALL AS THEY MAY.

* * *

The screen went blank.

"Well, at least we know we're dealing with an American," Agent Jacks said.

Kalista rubbed her brother's shoulders. "Were you able to locate the hacker's position?"

"I tried everything, sis—came close a couple of times, but crashed and burned every time. This particular worm and the encrypted firewalls fortifying it moved in a pattern I've never seen before."

"What's the status as of now?" Kalista asked Jacks.

"Ma'am, we're back on line and systems are functioning normally."

"Looks like we all need a vacation, wouldn't you say?"

"Yes, ma'am."

* * *

As the helicopters ascended in a V-formation, Riondro watched them go. "It never stops, does it?"

Kalista snuggled under his shoulder. "Thimpkin warned us that defending the world would be a daunting task."

"And he didn't lie. Are you ready to save the world, Major Flaker, leader of The Order?"

Kalista smiled. "I live for this shit. Rotten apple, remember?"

"I do, indeed."

They both smiled.

Epilogue

Walker ducked out through the swinging doors, leaving the screams and gunfire behind. He strolled down the hallway, enjoying his cigarette.

After a few minutes, Ingro met Walker in the hallway. Walker's point man picked flesh and bone from his uniform. "Mission accomplished, sir."

"You have an hour to get this place in order," Walker said. "And get yourself cleaned up. I won't have that filth inside my limousine."

"Of course, sir."

* * *

This was a type of silence that reeked of death. Death emanated from the dozens of bodies strewn about, their blood smeared violently in puddles and splatters. It was an image from a gothic mural of a ritualistic aftermath. Even a single intake of air meant boldly defying everything death meant.

Dr. Harold Grog moved his head ever so slightly—an act that proved a major feat given the unorthodox condition of his body. It was such a special hell to know anatomy at that moment! Grog felt the three distinct bullet wounds to his cranium, and with them, the knowledge that he had been struck through the left temporal, lower left cerebellum, and the upper parietal bone. With a force similar to that of a sledgehammer to the back of a skull as one lay face down on concrete—like being nailed to the floor—his face had been pressed down in the crevice of a small stair step, the second of three that connected to the stage in the conference room of this massive facility. He moved painfully in the three to four ounces of his and some of his colleague's coagulating blood.

He felt the condition of his body, but no pain. As his eyes began to dance about, he contemplated his circumstance. He noticed the sizable hole in the stair step his face had been buried in. He figured that with the shot he took to his upper parietal bone, the bullet must have traveled straight through, piercing the sphenoidal air sinus, the middle and inferior concha, shattering his hard palate, and forming the miniature crater he was about to drown in.

His body was grotesquely slumped over the destroyed torso of a fellow scientist. As Grog attempted to shake life into his limbs, an onslaught of pain suddenly seized him in its medieval grasp, causing him to scream from within.

Though the pain was unbearable, he tried to focus on what he knew to be reality. That what was taking place within him was really of his own design, and that the pain was simply an indicator that the seemingly archaic process was reaching its climax. His body remained dead to the world, but he knew that he was coming back. After all, he had run the tests. He knew all the scenarios. He anticipated this outcome and so realized that in this, the closest step ever reached in the succession of a perfect serum, he became what he never thought he would be: a perfect creation of his own design.

He watched in agony as his acidic blood chewed away at the bullets buried in his legs, cranium, chest, and back, into liquid. He endured as his internal organs rebuilt themselves before death released him from his momentary paralysis. He sat upright, looking around the room saddened at the carnage before him. He had to be patient, waiting for the strength to stand, to escape. If the soldiers performed their usual acid wash over the compound, he would be destroyed. But if not, he would ensure that Damion Walker would pay dearly for what he had done. He waited.

Acknowledgments

I am more grateful than I can say for the assistance of many people throughout my life who have helped me to learn and analyze the overwhelming amounts of information found within the pages of world history; from college professors to the librarians who tolerated my rather persistent questions pertaining to historical theory and events. However, in this project of mine there are some details which I have chosen to use—particularly with regard to certain theories and the timing of certain sites and events—which may not be accepted by the majority of the world at this time. This was done deliberately as I strategically weaved fact and fiction into a tapestry of historical information to present a backdrop to this monumental series.

Thanks to my first editor, Ms. Sammie Justesen, for helping me see the cracks in the wall I was continually banging my head against earlier in the game, and for bearing with me as trying times were literally kicking me in the ass. To my second editor, Ms. Serenity J. Banks, for providing a second pair of eyes to this project, and to Mr. Michael Garrett—credited as Stephen King's first editor—for his spot-on critique. Sir, what I took from that critique were tools that I'll continue to use with every project. I thank you all with everything I'm worth, for I'll never forget the editors and the book doctor who made an author of me.

Most especially, I want to thank my anonymous source for providing me with strong enough ammunition to objectively examine the American government, providing me the tools needed to creatively expose the hidden evils brewing within. You've provided this rather subjective novelist, one who must write about people with an understanding of human nature and the logical motivation for their actions, with an outlet so that I could shine a light on cloaked governmental pandemonium.

CPSIA information can be obtained at www.ICGtesting.com
Printed in the USA
BVOW04s1404140813

328572BV00001B/18/P